### Killing Spree

Hider spurred his horse in close, skidded it to a stop, and fired his .50-caliber into Sam's chest. The impact of the huge bullet blew the man backward. Then Hider swung his horse around with his knees, drew a large knife from inside his shirt, and threw it.

Slocum was never sure where it came from. The knife went up to the hilt into Gopher's chest.

Gopher staggered around in a circle, gurgling, holding the knife handle, unable to extract it. Finally, Hider booted his horse in and gave the man a shove forward with his moccasin. The man fell facedown and babbled his last.

# DON'T MISS THESE
## ALL-ACTION WESTERN SERIES
## FROM THE BERKLEY PUBLISHING GROUP

### THE GUNSMITH by J. R. Roberts
Clint Adams was a legend among lawmen, outlaws, and ladies. They called him . . . the Gunsmith.

### LONGARM by Tabor Evans
The popular long-running series about Deputy U.S. Marshal Custis Long—his life, his loves, his fight for justice.

### SLOCUM by Jake Logan
Today's longest-running action Western. John Slocum rides a deadly trail of hot blood and cold steel.

### BUSHWHACKERS by B. J. Lanagan
An action-packed series by the creators of Longarm! The rousing adventures of the most brutal gang of cutthroats ever assembled—Quantrill's Raiders.

### DIAMONDBACK by Guy Brewer
Dex Yancey is Diamondback, a Southern gentleman turned con man when his brother cheats him out of the family fortune. Ladies love him. Gamblers hate him. But nobody pulls one over on Dex . . .

### WILDGUN by Jack Hanson
The blazing adventures of mountain man Will Barlow—from the creators of Longarm!

### TEXAS TRACKER by Tom Calhoun
J.T. Law: the most relentless—and dangerous—manhunter in all Texas. Where sheriffs and posses fail, he's the best man to bring in the most vicious outlaws—for a price.

# JAKE LOGAN

## SLOCUM
## AND
## BELLE STARR

JOVE BOOKS, NEW YORK

**THE BERKLEY PUBLISHING GROUP**
**Published by the Penguin Group**
**Penguin Group (USA) Inc.**
**375 Hudson Street, New York, New York 10014, USA**

Penguin Group (Canada), 90 Eglinton Avenue East, Suite 700, Toronto, Ontario M4P 2Y3, Canada
(a division of Pearson Penguin Canada Inc.)
Penguin Books Ltd., 80 Strand, London WC2R 0RL, England
Penguin Group Ireland, 25 St. Stephen's Green, Dublin 2, Ireland (a division of Penguin Books Ltd.)
Penguin Group (Australia), 250 Camberwell Road, Camberwell, Victoria 3124, Australia
(a division of Pearson Australia Group Pty. Ltd.)
Penguin Books India Pvt. Ltd., 11 Community Centre, Panchsheel Park, New Delhi—110 017, India
Penguin Group (NZ), 67 Apollo Drive, Rosedale, North Shore 0632, New Zealand
(a division of Pearson New Zealand Ltd.)
Penguin Books (South Africa) (Pty.) Ltd., 24 Sturdee Avenue, Rosebank, Johannesburg 2196,
South Africa

Penguin Books Ltd., Registered Offices: 80 Strand, London WC2R 0RL, England

This is a work of fiction. Names, characters, places, and incidents either are the product of the author's imagination or are used fictitiously, and any resemblance to actual persons, living or dead, business establishments, events, or locales is entirely coincidental.

SLOCUM AND BELLE STARR

A Jove Book / published by arrangement with the author

PRINTING HISTORY
Jove edition / October 2009

Copyright © 2009 by Penguin Group (USA) Inc.
Cover illustration by Sergio Giovine.

ISBN: 978-0-515-14726-1

JOVE®
Jove Books are published by The Berkley Publishing Group,
a division of Penguin Group (USA) Inc.
375 Hudson Street, New York, New York 10014.
JOVE® is a registered trademark of Penguin Group (USA) Inc.
The "J" design is a trademark of Penguin Group (USA) Inc.

PRINTED IN THE UNITED STATES OF AMERICA

10  9  8  7  6  5  4  3  2  1

# 1

The mare he'd bought off a farmer back about Conway, Arkansas, had begun favoring her right hind foot. By the road signs, Slocum still lacked sixty miles of reaching Fort Smith. That meant he still had two more days of travel on this boggy river road the U.S. Army Corps of Engineers had originally built following the Arkansas River to Fort Smith. His luck with horses the past two weeks had all been bad. The gelding he'd bought near Memphis had had to be destroyed at the Conway livery the night before. Took the colic on moldy grain—but it was no great loss. He was a spindly legged horse that the man who sold him claimed to be a fast stake racer. That was a lie, unless he'd run him against pissants.

The mid-morning sun peered down through the small leaves on the tall oak, hickory, and ash trees that lined the road. Up until then, his ride had been a pleasant one. A stagecoach had passed him earlier, the driver charging through like his tail was on fire and the tipsy coach rocking from side to side as he flew eastward. Slocum had passed several freighters and farmers hauling produce to market, a buggy or two, and even some rigs drawn by oxen. This was the main route east to west—so badly rutted in places that he'd tried to avoid them, but in some cases had been forced to cross the muddy spots because of farmers' split-rail fences that limited the width of the right-of-way.

New corn and cotton crops were emerging. This soil was not the rich delta land of eastern Arkansas. The farms he passed looked to be still recovering from the conflict that only very recently had swept though this river bottom during the bitter war.

With the mare giving in to that hind foot, he knew he would need a new mount if he was ever to reach the Indian Territory. In another mile, at the rate she was favoring it, he'd be off her and walking. He stopped beside the road and dismounted to check the ailing hoof again.

A well-dressed young woman driving a fine horse and buggy reined up beside him. Her dark eyes flashed like chunks of coal and she had a friendly, melodious voice. "Are you having trouble with your horse, sir?"

He dropped the hoof and raised up to speak to her. "She's sprained her right ankle or has something. I can't find a thing in her hoof."

"That's a shame. Hitch her on the back and get in my buggy. I'll take you to the nearest place where you can find help or a new horse."

"Why, ma'am," he said removing his hat, "that would be mighty kind of you doing that for a stranger. My name's Slocum."

"Well, Mr. Slocum, my name's Mrs. Myrabelle Younger. My good friends call me Belle."

"Slocum's fine. This isn't putting you out of your way, is it?"

"Lands, no. I'm going to Fort Smith."

"All right, I'll hitch her on behind. My luck with horses this past week has not been good."

She laughed freely at his words as he went by her to hitch the mare on. When the mare was tied to the tailgate, he came around the buggy and met the woman face to face. The cowboy hat she wore with the brim pinned back by a large feather looked unique, but it suited her. He also noted she wore a large-caliber six-gun in a holster around her waist. She might be a young lady, but obviously she was taking no chances on road agents or horny men attacking her.

For a long moment, she didn't move, examining him from top to bottom like a horse buyer, before she scooted aside for him with a mischievous smile and let him join her. When he was on the seat, she took up the reins and sitting straight-backed, clucked to her horse. The good-looking bay stepped out smartly and Slocum, starting to relax, sat back on the padded horsehair seat beside her. Belle must have some money from the looks of this rig along with her black satin jacket and long skirt. Buttoned-up leather shoes peeked out from under the hem. They might even have been made from expensive dog skin.

"Where do you live, Slocum?" she asked.

He made a grin. "Under the stars."

"You are from the South. I recognize the accent."

"I am. Before the war. Georgia."

"I use to live in Carthage, Missouri, back then, but the Damnyankees have taken over all that country." She reined her horse around a mud hole and back on the road again. He leaned around the buggy top and checked on the mare. Without the weight of a rider, she traveled well enough to keep up.

"She all right?"

"Coming on fine." He settled back in the seat.

"Good. I now live down on the Canadian River about seventy-five miles from Fort Smith."

"You and your husband farm?"

"Mostly we trade horses."

"I see."

"So you have no wife? Nor a fine bottomland farm?"

"None of the above."

"What do you do for a living?"

"Try to get by. I gamble some. I'm headed for Texas. I understand that the cattle drives to Kansas are making some money this year. I thought I might hook up with one of them."

"Since they aren't going up through the Ozark Mountains, they may well work. Those bald knobbers and outlaw gangs up there robbed and raided so many of those first drives to Sedalia last year."

He nodded. She not only was pert and attractive, but very well educated. Interesting woman, and he was moving in the direction he wanted to go. From Fort Smith, he planned on taking the old Butterfield Road down to Fort Worth. If he could ride that far with her, surely he could find a sound horse in a town as big as Fort Smith. Besides that, he rather liked her company.

"Is your husband expecting you back?"

She turned and blinked her eyes at him. "Oh, we are—temporarily separated, I might say. He's gone to Nebraska for a while on—business. But he'll be back. Do you know him?"

"What's his name?" He decided that she sure didn't lie very well about her marriage arrangement.

After a quick check around to be sure that they were alone, she held her left gloved hand next to her mouth and whispered, "Cole Younger."

"We've met."

"Oh, then when he returns, I shall tell him I've met you." With the reins, she slapped the horse to increase his trot. "I know now that you gamble and you are going to Texas. I lived east of Dallas toward the last end of the war, and my parents still live down there on a farm. Bustling place."

"I was raised up farming, too." He looked over the fields of emerging crops on both sides of the road. "I hope I never have to touch another boll of cotton or shuck of corn ever again."

"I have to say the same thing. Have you ever been to the west coast? Do you know what California is like?"

He nodded. "I've been out there. Different than the South. Nice climate. Lots of fruit. Things are very expensive. That's left over from the gold rush, I expect. They had no war out there. None of their farms and land were laid to waste."

She nodded. "I think I would like to go see it sometime."

"Not my kinda country. Did you see those huge dead trees and the charred ruins of that large home place back there?" he asked. The looks of the burned-down mansion made his stomach curdle and a sourness crawl up his throat.

"Yes."

"Those are the scars of the South that I'm not sure will ever heal."

"You are right. The hotel and the livery my father once owned in Carthage lie in ashes today." She drew her shoulders back and forced her breasts against the front of the jacket. "Gawdamn them Yankees anyway."

"Amen," he said.

"I have some relatives ahead at Coal Hill. They're Shirleys. My father's side of the house. Perhaps we can stop there tonight. They may even know of a good horse for sale."

"Ma'am, I sure don't want to trouble you any more than I have to."

"Trouble me?" She reached over and squeezed the top of his leg familiarly. "Why, darling, you are not troubling me one little bit. I was bored plumb to death driving this buggy all alone. Fact is that we can wait until Fort Smith or Alma to find you that horse."

"Make it easy on yourself."

She looked sideways at him and smiled as if that pleased her. "I shall. When we get across this creek coming up, let us stop and have some lunch. Jasper could stand a little rest and your mare probably will be grateful. I have some bread and cold cuts and cheese."

"It sounds wonderful."

"Why, then, we'll just do that."

The buggy wheels sliced through the shallow crossing, and Jasper, her buggy horse, easily climbed up on the flat beside the road. She stopped him in the shade of the big white oaks.

"Want him unhooked?" Slocum asked.

"Sure, and I'll prepare our picnic."

He undid the harness and then led Jasper and the sore-footed mare over to some new grass they could reach, and hitched them there to a rail fence. He walked back and discovered she had unfurled a blanket and was setting out the lunch. Her neatness about the way she did things intrigued him. How did she and Cole Younger get tied up? Not that he blamed Younger, but why did such a much-wanted outlaw marry a young lady of her obvious class? On the other hand, Slocum decided, sitting down across from her, why did a woman with such education and manners want to marry a wanted man? No telling.

She began buttering and then putting mustard on the slice of bread in her hand. Next, she piled several thin slices of beef roast on the bread and stacked some dry cheese on top of that. "I hope this suits you, Slocum."

"Ma'am, it looks fit for a king."

"I have some cool lemonade also." She placed the sandwich on a cloth napkin, rose, and holding up her skirts, went to the buggy. She returned, carrying a crock jug in her arm and smiled at him. "Sorry, there is no whiskey in this one."

"Lemonade's fine."

"If it's sweet enough?" She paused, waiting for his answer.

"If it's sweet enough, yes."

"Women can be like lemonade. Sharp, but when sweetened, they are all right, aren't they?"

"Yes, ma'am."

"You know, I see in your eyes that you leave many things unsaid. Do you know that?" She poured him some lemonade in a cup and handed it to him. "How is that?"

He took a large sip and nodded in approval. "Ah, great."

"Good. Give me the cup back so I may fill it. I wasn't going to waste it on you if you didn't like it."

"A minute ago you mentioned seeing things in me."

She set the jug down, handed him the cup of lemonade, and then scooted over in front of him on her knees. "Maybe if you kiss me, that will open up those secrets."

He caught her face in his palms and kissed her hard. Her arms flew around his neck and he soon tasted her flashing tongue. He closed his eyes, enjoying her hot, hungry mouth.

Out of breath, she settled back on her heels and took a deep breath. "We can't stop at my Uncle Jack Shirley's place tonight. I am afraid we'd keep everyone up for hours with all the noise we'd make in bed together."

"Whatever you say. I'm just along for the ride, ma'am."

"Oh, we had better eat now." Her eyes glistened. "I can even see where we may never get to Fort Smith."

"Oh, we'll make it there somehow."

She shook her head warily. "I don't think we will ever get there." Searching around, she grimaced at the sight of some passing wagons on the nearby road. Then she gritted her teeth. "This place is sure not the site to do anything about it. Is it? But trust me, I shall find us a secluded place. Oh, I'm sorry—" She ran her palm down his cheek and looked hard into his eyes. "How mean of me to forget that I was feeding you."

He took her sandwich and at the first bite, the saliva flooded his mouth. Whether it was from considering what her breasts would taste like or from the bread and meat, he wasn't certain. But between then and dark, he had faith that she'd find them a secluded enough place where he could uncover the answer.

# 2

The sign said one mile to Woodson Church and Cemetery, with an arrow to the north. They'd turned down the narrow country lane in search of some privacy.

"I think that churchyard may be where we stay tonight," Belle said, nestled under his right arm as she let him drive Jasper. She had stolen an occasional kiss, and now pressed his palm to the jacket material over her right breast. When he tweaked it, she grinned up at him. "See, I am a real woman."

He shook his head and continued to drive Jasper up the country lane. "How would I know that?"

"Well, you will have to find out when the sun goes down."

"But I want to see you in the daylight."

She slumped in a pout. "Maybe when I know you better we can do that. Right now, I'd feel funny if it was in the daylight and you were staring at me all naked."

"I'd bet you're pretty in the buff."

"You say I'd look like a bluff?"

He looked at the roof of the buggy over them for help. "I said you'd look—"

She rose up and kissed him in the face. Hugging his neck, she stopped and made a funny face while looking back down the narrow road. "We have some company. It looks like the law."

She quickly settled her skirt and sat back down without her arm around him. It was like she had something to hide. He couldn't figure out why two lawmen would bother her.

"Law?" he asked under his breath.

"Yes, two men who are dressed in suits. They look like lawmen and are pointing at us. You do anything wrong back there?"

"No, ma'am," he said.

She huddled on the seat with her hands in her lap as if waiting for the inevitable as he reined Jasper over to the side of the road. What in the hell did lawmen want with them anyway?

Slocum stopped the horse to await their arrival. Why would—

The mustached, long-faced man rode up next to the buggy with his partner beside him. He took off his big hat when he saw Belle. "Howdy, I'm Deputy Ruff Carr from Faulkner County, Arkansas. We're looking for a mare that was stolen in my jurisdiction."

"I have a bill of sale for the one tied on behind," Slocum said.

"Mind showing me?" Carr asked, taking out his reading glasses from inside his suit coat pocket.

Slocum dismounted from the buggy and nodded to the other solemn-looking lawman riding with Carr. He drew the sale paper drawn from his vest pocket, unfolded it, and handed it to Carr.

Carr studied it, then read it aloud. "One bay mare, four years old, scar on inside of right front leg, no brand, is sold by Nathan Godfrey owner free of all liens and title. Signed Nathan Godfrey and today's date."

Carr held out the paper toward the other man. "You want to read it, Sims?"

"No." The man shook his head.

"Sorry to bother you, mister," Carr said. "You too, Mrs. . . ."

"Mrs. Slocum," she said.

"Well, you two go on now. We thought we'd run onto a horse that had recently been stolen in my district. Sorry to bother you."

"No problem," Slocum said, and got back on the seat and clucked to Jasper.

When they were up the road a little ways, she turned and looked back. "Those two no-good sons a bitches are up to something. What was it? They were no more looking for a stolen horse than the man in the moon."

"Maybe they wanted to meet my new wife," Slocum teased.

She ignored his words, still fuming. "I hate them worthless badge toters worse than I do a copperhead snake in my garden. Sneaking around all the time and acting like you'd stolen that mare. Makes me so gawdamn mad."

"Hey, they're gone. They never did anything but looked us over."

"They wanted something. If I could put my finger on it, I'd sure like to know—"

He bent over and kissed her. In an instant, she threw her arms around his neck and furiously kissed him back. When she got mad, she sure got heated up as well. It was a real shame, Slocum thoguht, that ole Cole was in Nebraska.

Why didn't he believe she really was married to Younger? What difference did it make? Maybe those two lawmen thought he was Cole Younger and had stopped them to check him out. No telling. He was more interested in this fiery woman and her body than anything else at the moment.

She half stood up, looking things over. "There's the small church and cemetery. Pull around back out of sight. Just like I thought it would be. No one is around."

He agreed, and drove the rig behind the small clapboard

schoolhouse-church. Standing on the ground, he took her by the waist and lifted her off the buggy, ending up in a big embrace with him kissing her some more.

While she was in his arms and being held off the ground, she swept her long black hair over her shoulders and smiled at him. "I swear, Slocum, you must be a man in a great need."

He swung her around. "Now why do you say that?"

"Well, between you and me, I can feel that large root that is the cause." Then she took off her hat and threw her head back. "I could howl like a coyote over finding you today, do you know that?"

"No, ma'am, but I'm plumb grateful you stopped." He lowered her to the ground and she went to take the blanket off the seat.

"I swear, Slocum, if I get eat up from chiggers—"

"Let's see if the church is unlocked."

"Good idea. You check. I need to use the outhouse."

"Sure," he said, and let her go to the raw wood facility made out of sawmill slabs.

Around in front, he found both church doors padlocked. As he came back down the side, he found an unlocked window he could open. He put his elbows on the sill, then with some effort, managed to wiggle inside and spill out on the floor. He reset the Colt he wore and rose to his feet. Then he went to the back door and unbolted it.

When he stuck his head out, she was standing by the outhouse, hands on her hips, looking around for him.

"Over here," he hissed, not knowing why he was being so quiet.

When she arrived with her blanket, he shook his head at her. "They have the front door locked. I had to come in through a window."

"Folks must be edgy around here, locking a church and all."

On the blackboard was a message from John 3:16.

"For God so loved the world that he gave his only begotten son, so who so ever believed in him shall have everlasting life," she recited. "I learned that a long time ago in Bible school."

Then, seeing the upright piano, she walked over and tested a few keys. She made a sour face at their response, then as if on a whim, she swept her skirt underneath her, sat down, and began to play "Swing Low, Sweet Chariot." The music filled the small church and she sang a few choruses. Next, her long fingers played a Chopin waltz, and he took a seat on the bench beside her with his arm hugging her shoulder as she worked the keyboard and he enjoyed the entertainment and their closeness. He wished someone else could play so she could dance and swirl across the floor in his arms.

"Wonderful music," he said at the end, impressed by her talent.

She turned and kissed him. "But you didn't come in here to hear my poor piano playing, did you?"

"To be honest, no, I did not. But I still enjoyed it very much."

She slowly unbuttoned the jacket in the shadowy light coming from outside. "Clouds must be gathering."

He agreed as he watched her open the blouse she wore underneath the jacket to expose her cup-sized breasts capped with pointed brown nipples on a sea of pearl white skin. He reached over and cupped the left one in his hand. Then he bend down to kiss her mouth as he savored the touch of her flesh and felt his excitement rising.

She tore his mouth away. "You ain't disappointed in them, are you?"

"Lord, no, you're lovely." He leaned over and tasted the left breast.

She clamped him to it and pressed it hard at him. His tongue's action raised her nipple to rock hardness. Her hand soon discovered his erection under his pants, and she gasped at her discovery, but that didn't stop her from rubbing the material on top of it.

"We need to get shed of some firearms," he whispered in her ear.

"But I might want to shoot you," she teased, and then stood up undoing her gun belt.

"You'll have plenty of time to shoot me after we to do it," he said, taking off his own.

She walked over and shook out her blanket on the floor. Then, taking a seat on it, she began using a shoe hook to unbutton her footgear. "These damn things take forever to undo if you're in a hurry."

He toed his own boots away and stripped off his shirt. He placed it on top of his Colt on the bench and then began to shed his britches.

"Sorry I'm so damn slow, but I'll catch up with you," she said, working on the second shoe with her bare legs tucked under her chin. "This floor will be kinda hard to do it on."

She stopped and tested the floor with the heel of her palm. At last, the second shoe was off and she rose to wiggle down the skirt, stopping with it halfway off her hips. "You sure you want to do this?"

He stepped in and kissed her.

Then, out of breath, she said, "I'll unwrap it for you to see me."

The skirt and blouse were tossed aside, and he swept her in his arms and her hand rushed down to squeeze his rising cock.

"Let's lie down," she whispered and soon was on her back with him kneeling before her. She drew her snowy knees up, then quickly spread them apart for his entry and reached down to guide his shaft in her slick gates.

"Easy," she gasped as he pumped it into her. When he penetrated her ring of fire, she made a moan. His ass wanted to poke his aching dick out the other side, but he managed to maintain control, and soon pushed his way through the muscular collar in gentle strokes that aroused a fever in her.

Savoring her, he plunged deep inside, and his muscle-corded belly bounced against hers with each drive. He held himself up so as not to crush her, and enjoyed watching the dizzy look gather in her eyes and the head-tossing that soon covered her face with a veil of her long thick hair.

His actions began to cause contractions inside her that made her raise her butt off the blanket to meet his every thrust. They both became lost in a whirlpool of fiery desire that suspended them over a deep canyon, and then they began to fall earthward. Seconds later, he came inside her with the force of one of those gold-sluicing operations in California. She sighed and collapsed in a soft faint.

Then, clearing the hair away from her face, she sat up halfway, bracing her arms behind her when he went back on his heels. "I know now," she said. "Those gawdamn no-good sons a bitches thought you might be Cole Younger, didn't they? That was not any fucking horse deal at all. They were not after that mare one little bit. It was Cole they wanted, wasn't it?"

"That makes sense."

She lay back down and swept the hair from her forehead one-handed. "Let's do that again. This time I'll pay more attention to you, darling. Those no-good . . ."

Maybe solving the mystery of the lawmen made her fiercer the second time, because she really raised her butt off the floor and met his every thrust, open mouthed and moaning in pleasure's arms. When he finally came, she collapsed and hugged him hard to her.

"Sweet Jesus, you are great fun. I just wish I had you in a goose-down bed—" Thunder cut her words off, and he smiled.

Then reality struck him and he rose up in disgust. "We'd better get our things inside. It's going to storm."

"Oh, damn. I hate these shoes."

"Stay in here. I'll bring it all in. It won't take me long."

She frowned with concern at him. "Aw, I hate to do that to you."

He hurriedly dressed. "Don't hate anything you've done to me."

In a hurry, he kissed her and then ran outside.

Before he had all her cases, her sidesaddle, and her boxes inside, large cold drops began to soak through his shirt. Then he tossed his war bag and bedroll inside, and ran back to unsaddle the mare between bolts of nearby lightning streaks that made the air stink of sulfur. When the mare was at last hitched beside the unharnessed Jasper, he sloshed across the yard, wet to the skin, and went inside the church, lamenting to himself how he'd forgotten to put on his canvas coat, which was inside the bedroll.

Strains of "Amazing Grace" came from the piano in the darkened room. The windows flashed with blinding lightning, thunder shook the floor, and the incessant drum of the heavy rain with some hail on the shake roof roared outside in the midst of a furious storm. Yet her silhouette as she sat straight-backed on the bench playing the ivory keys brought a knot to his throat he couldn't swallow. *How great thou art . . . how great thou art.*

# 3

The cold air in the room caused goose bumps to form on his wet skin and made him shiver. When she discovered his condition, she stopped playing the piano despite his protests, and stripped off his wet clothing and unwrapped his bedroll. They climbed inside to drive the chill out of him. Under the covers, she undressed, and soon her warm flesh pressed to his cold skin was stopping his shivering. He enjoyed her attention and the closeness. Squeezing her firm butt and rubbing his palm over her lower belly, he soon began probing her with his finger, and she quickly grew excited. Raised up, she sprawled on top of him and pushed her muff hard against his leg.

Then she swept her hair back from her face, and laughed. "You are really one horny fella. How long has it been since you've had any?"

"I forgot."

She tapped him on the end of his nose. "That's going to grow five inches if you tell any more lies."

He lifted her up and began to feast on her breasts. It was heady business, and outside, the storm roared even louder.

"Is there a cellar around here? Anywhere we can get into until this storm is over?" she asked, listening to the monsters tearing at the building. "This kind of weather is going to turn up tornados."

"I know, it might. But when it's your time, in a cellar or not, death's going to get you."

"But—but I don't like to take unnecessary chances on that sort of thing. Man, it is really storming outside now."

He reached underneath her and with her assistance, inserted his dick in her cunt again. She arched her back and braced herself above him to work it. "We might as well do this. I guess I would rather die screwing you to death as sit around and hold hands with a bunch of crybabies in a 'fraidy hole."

They both laughed.

By morning, the storm had passed. They finished the last of her bread and meat for breakfast. He went out through the wet grass and harnessed Jasper in the first light. Then, as she packed things and rolled up their bedroll, he began to carry everything out to put in the buggy.

"Oh." He stopped in the doorway. "Don't you come out here. I'll carry you to the buggy. You'll ruin your good shoes walking in all this water and wet grass."

"Well, ain't you the gentleman. Slocum, you are mighty polite worrying about my shoes. Most men would not have even noticed them."

"I'm not most men. I noticed them all right."

"By the way, you are not like most men I have known either."

"Good. When I get it all done, I'll come for you."

"Very well, I shall play a Strauss waltz for you while I wait on your gallant offer."

At last, with everything loaded and with her gathered up in his arms to keep her shoes dry, she pulled the back door shut after them and he carried her over to the buggy. Once they were on it, she turned and squeezed his face to kiss him. "You are the nicest man I have ever had an affair with. I shall not forget you."

He glanced at the mare tied behind and then took his seat. He slapped Jasper lightly on the butt and they were off, with Mrs. Younger squeezing his arm to death.

"Maybe we could go to California?" she suggested.

He made a face at her. "I've been there. Don't like it out there."

When they were on the Fort Smith Road at last, the ruts were underwater in places from all the rain. He held Jasper down to a light trot, and in many places let him walk around the worst of it all.

They crossed some murky roiling creek that clearly flowed much higher than it had the day before.

"Look." She pointed to a large downed shade tree in a yard they passed that had been splintered off. "A tornado did that last night. See how it was twisted off at the base? We were lucky."

He laughed. "Next time it storms, we'll stay upstairs again. I liked it much better than them old spider holes they call cellars."

Shaking her head, she punched him on the arm. "You liked it all right."

"You didn't like it?" He blinked in make-believe shock at her.

Her long dark lashes narrowed at him. "Aren't you even sore this morning?"

"Why, no."

She rolled her eyes and looked for help to the thick clouds passing quickly over them.

At mid-morning, they stopped at her Uncle John Shirley's fine house in Coal Hill. It was a two-storied whitewashed clapboard structure with a wide covered porch around two sides.

"Listen to me. For the next thirty minutes you are Cole Younger," she said under her breath as she got down from the buggy. "They don't know him or you, and I want them to think that's who you are." She paused, hitting her hat on the buggy roof.

He put a finger to her mouth. "Just don't overdo it?"

She looked anxiously at the house. "I'll try not to."

Her uncle came out and rushed down the stairs from the porch with a newspaper in his hand. "Myrabelle Shirley, why, it's you," he said, and embraced her.

"Uncle John, I want you to meet my husband, Cole Younger."

"Well, sir, you have married my favorite niece." He looked around in mild shock. "Where's your baby?" he asked her.

"Darling Pearl is at home. I have a black woman nursing her and she couldn't make the trip to Nashville."

"I was hoping to get to see her. So was your aunt."

"How is Aunt Mona?" she asked.

"Weak, but she remains determined. Let's go inside and introduce your Mr. Younger to her. I am certain she'd like to meet this strapping young man who married her favorite niece." He clapped Slocum on the arm. "Come in. I'll fix some fresh coffee. Did you two have breakfast?"

"Yes, sir, thanks. We've had breakfast."

"May I call you Cole?" John asked.

"Sure."

Belle hugged Slocum's arm and smiled with pride as he went along with her farce. They followed her uncle inside the spacious house.

"You sure have a fine place here," Slocum said, looking around.

"The Damnyankees used it for their headquarters during the war. I guess that's all that saved it from the torch."

"You were lucky."

"Mona and I both were in Texas at the time with Belle's parents. A former slave, Ishaid, who'd stayed here also looked after it until we got back. He saved it many times from being razed and torn down. The KKK almost hung him for his stubborn insistence that we'd be coming back for it."

Slocum nodded. They went into a bright downstairs bedroom, and propped up on the bed was a pale-faced woman who smiled warmly when she saw them.

"Why, Myrabelle, darling, you have grown into such a lovely lady."

"Aunt Mona, I want you to meet Cole Younger, my husband."

The woman held out her veined hand and Slocum stepped in and kissed it.

"Oh, how gallant of you, Cole. I may call you Cole?"

"Yes, ma'am."

"Thank you. Myrabelle, I can see you have done so well finding, not only a handsome strapping man, but a Southern gentleman as well."

Belle nodded, taking a seat. "You two go make coffee. Aunt Mona and I should talk."

"I'd say we were being run out, sir," John said, and the two men excused themselves.

Once in the kitchen, John stoked the range with sticks of wood and filled a coffeepot from a bucket of water.

"Well, sir, what is your business?"

"I'm—we're on our way to Fort Worth. I may find a herd of cattle to take to Kansas this summer."

"Is that profitable?"

"People are making money, they say. There's a new railroad shipping point at Abilene, Kansas, sounds like it is working much better than the Sedalia drives. A man named Joe McCoy seems to have things up there in good order, from the reports I have heard."

"Driving cattle from Texas to Kansas. My, my, that sounds like a terribly dangerous journey through the Indian Territory and all."

Slocum sat in the chair John offered him. "There isn't much of anything else to do. I don't want to farm, so I better sharpen my skills at cattle driving."

"I wish you the best of luck. Is she staying down on the Canadian River with the baby?"

"I don't know yet."

"Wonderful girl. Has she played the piano for you?"

Slocum nodded. "She's very talented."

"The war and all. She ran messages to our forces, you know, during the war? I think the excitement and all made her restless. I hope for your sake, now that she has the baby, that she settles down and accepts her role as a mother and a wife with you and Baby Pearl."

Slocum nodded, and folded and unfolded his hands on the tabletop. "It has been trying times for many of us. I'm sure she will find herself."

"You are what she needed, a strong man." John reached over while standing up and clapped Slocum on the shoulder before answering the call of the boiling water to add the ground coffee. Though Slocum was going to learn shortly that that it wasn't coffee at all, but rather scorched ground barley. Uncle John, like so many other once-rich Southerners, was skimping to get by on his meager finances. Things weren't fair in life, and had turned out even worse after Lee surrendered.

The day proceeded, and that evening Slocum and Belle were in the bed on the back porch listening to the whippoorwill calls. Belle was half sprawled on his chest as she said in his ear, "Thank you. Thank you for not fussing about his terrible barley coffee. Thank you for not giving away my secret, too. You are a true friend and gentleman."

Her nimble fingers began to stir his dick to awareness.

"I thought you were sore," he said, teasing her.

"Not after all you did for me today." She kissed him. "It's the only way I can pay you back. I have no money."

"Mr. John. Mr. John." A black man was at the back door around the corner, calling to her uncle and sounding upset.

Slocum sat up and quickly pulled on his pants.

"I'm coming, Ishaid," John shouted out to the man.

"Hurry, Mr. John, you's got big troubles."

Slocum was barefoot on the smooth porch flooring, and was buttoning his shirt when he reached the corner.

"Come in, Ishaid," John said, and pulled the man into the kitchen. "Whatever is wrong?"

Slocum edged toward the back door to overhear the conversation.

". . . why, yes, Cole Younger is here. Why?"

"Dey be talking down at the saloon tonight that he be here and they done sent for the deputy U.S. marshal from over at Ozark to come with them in the morning and arrest him. Says there be a five-hundred-dollar reward on him."

"That you, Cole?" John asked, not having lighted a lamp in the dark kitchen. "You hear what my good friend Ishaid said?"

"Yes. Were they deputy sheriffs from Conway?" Slocum asked.

"Yes, sah."

He didn't need to be arrested and investigated closely, even if he wasn't Cole Younger. The reward for him was much less, but still, he could face charges.

"What's wrong now?" Belle asked, rewrapped in the sheet. "Oh, is that you, Ishaid?"

"Yes, ma'am, I sure do wish, Miss Belle, I could hear you play that piano. You's sure be good at that."

"Carr and Sims have sent for a deputy U.S. marshal from over by Ozark to help them arrest me," Slocum said. Belle looked blank, then suddenly remembered that Slocum was pretending to be Cole Younger.

"Oh, what will we do?" She hugged Slocum's arm possessively.

"Get me a saddle horse and I'll get the hell out of here."

"Ishaid, who has a good saddle horse for sale?" John asked the black man.

"Mr. Paine, he's done got a real good'un."

"What will he take for it?" Belle asked, sounding suspicious of the deal.

"He say no less'n fifty dollars."

"That's way too damn much," she said, and dropped her head in disgusted defeat.

"Can you go buy that horse for fifty bucks, no questions asked?" Slocum asked.

"Yes, sah."

"Cole, excuse me," John said. "But Ishaid is a very good horse man. He says it is a good horse, you can count on it."

"Light a small candle," Slocum said to her.

She brought the lighted lamp over, and he counted out fifty dollars in gold and silver coins in the black man's palm. "Be quick, and don't let them know a thing."

"Yes, sah. No one will know a thing. Mr. Paine, he be a good man, too."

"For that much gawdamn money, he ought to be," Belle said in disgust, and blew out the candle.

"We have no time to argue or trade," Slocum said to her as Ishaid excused himself. "You be careful, too," Slocum said after the man.

"I know," she said, sounding annoyed. "Still, thirty dollars would buy a great stud horse today."

Slocum spoke up. "John, you may have that mare. She should get over being lame and make a good garden horse for you."

"Oh, Ishaid can cure most anything about a horse. How much did you pay for her? I'll write you a note for her."

Slocum shook his head in the weak moonlight streaming into the room, and hugged the sheet-wrapped Belle standing in front of him, rocking her a little from side to side. "The mare's a gift to you and him from us," he said to John.

"I can't accept such a gift."

"Yes, you can. She'll give you some transportation and with Ishaid, you can make a truck patch. It's still early enough to do that."

"Oh, God bless you, Cole Younger. My, my, Myrabelle, what a fine man you have chosen. I'll make us some coffee," John said.

Slocum would have rather had a shot of whiskey, but he could choke down one more cup of that bitter stuff. "I better get dressed and gather my stuff. How far away does this Paine live?"

"Only a few blocks," John said.

"Excuse me," Slocum said. He needed to get his things ready and get the hell out of there.

On the porch, she told him in a loud whisper, "I'm going, too. Jasper rides well and can jump fences."

"What about—what about Pearl?"

"My aunt has her. She will be fine. I am riding out with you. I can come back and get my buggy at some later time. Uncle John will keep it for me along with some other things I cannot pack with me. I will not be any burden to you."

"There really isn't room—I mean, on the dodge, you have to put in some long days and lots of hard riding."

Dressing in the shadowy light of the porch on the other side of their bed, she slapped her bare ass before wiggling up her skirt. "I have the ass for that."

She sure had the ass for other things, too, but to take a woman along on the run was something he'd never tried before up to this point in his life. He wouldn't even have considered anyone else. Belle Younger—Shirley, whatever—was no ordinary woman.

He finished dressing, and could hear a horse coming up the street in the starlight. Not an ordinary horse either. He sounded like a handful for the black man to lead. It was time for Slocum to decide about Belle. Take her along or leave her?

"This won't be no picnic," he said.

"You are not telling me a thing, darling, that I do not already know."

"Then get your things. We've got to get the hell out of here right now."

She rushed over and hugged him, then buried her face in his vest. "Oh, Slocum, you will never regret this. Not for one minute."

He better not—either. This could be serious. He hurried off to meet Ishaid, who obviously was having some problems controlling the spirited horse. Slocum took the lead on the halter. He damn sure was a tall horse and full of steam. Sixteen hands and excited. Slocum tied him close to the ring on the barn, then began brushing off his back to put on the saddle.

"He sure be a real horse," Ishaid said as John held the lamp up for Slocum to see what he was doing.

"He gave you and me that mare to garden with," John said to the black man.

"Oh, that be too good. I's go to sweating that leg and get dat limp out of her."

Slocum nodded while speaking to calm the Paine horse. He kept putting the saddle blanket on and taking if off to settle the horse. Then, finally, he went to patting the blanket down, and Belle carried his Texas saddle over to him.

"Is he rideable?" she asked, sounding concerned.

"He'll be a handful. It'll be fine. Jasper's saddled. I get this one cinched down, we're getting of out of here."

"I'll go get mounted?"

"Yes. I may need Jasper to be with him when I get on him. He's so damn high-headed."

"I understand," she said, and ran off to mount her horse.

When the saddle was on the Paine horse, Slocum cinched it up tight while Ishaid made new holes in the head stall to fit the animal. When the halter was off, the bit in his mouth, and the bridle on his head, Slocum sorted the leather reins, then clutched the horn and vaulted in the saddle. His toes sought the stirrups and, not seeing Belle, he turned the Paine horse right into her and Jasper.

"Sorry," Slocum said, sawing on the animal's jaw to get him in control and backing the big horse into the barn. Then the Paine horse bounced off the siding, which sent him forward, and Slocum wished he had spurs to punish the animal.

When he was ready to ride, Slocum nodded at Belle and led the way into the street. Then, beside him, Belle turned Jasper north toward the main road. As they galloped side by side under the starlight and in the shadowy darkness when they rode under the overhanging trees, the Paine horse only tried to buck once, but Slocum was able to contain him. The big gelding really wanted to race.

"Halt!" someone shouted, and ran out into the street to stop them. Before Slocum could stop her, Belle ran the man over with Jasper, knocking him aside like a bowling pin. Slocum let the Paine horse run faster to distance them from the man. Jasper and Belle kept up with him.

"Who in the hell was that?" she asked, looking back.

"I guess a guard they must have posted."

"Dumb fella thought he could stop us?"

Slocum nodded. The fool'd be lucky not to have broken bones.

They rounded a corner, and soon were out in the farmland, galloping west on the main road. A great horned owl swooped down, and then it soared back up in the night sky.

In a large mud hole that Jasper managed to skirt, the Paine horse lost his footing. Slocum managed to kick out of the stirrups. The gelding went down to his knees in a sea of muck, and came within inches of tossing Slocum over his head. But Slocum held his seat and was prepared for the powerful horse's recovery, in a furious scramble to his feet that sent wet crud flying in every direction as the horse came lunging out of the mess. Tasting the sour gritty mud in his own mouth, Slocum reined the horse up as Belle rode back.

"You all right?" she asked.

"Yes. We need to slow down some. That would have been a wreck with an ordinary horse."

"I'll watch closer," she promised, and they moved out in a long trot. By dawn, they had passed many camps along the road with travelers rising for the day. The smoke of cooking fires, the smell of bacon frying, and other familiar odors made Slocum's stomach roil. But there was no time to stop and eat.

"See those mountains to the north?" She pointed them out. "I think we can find us a place to hide for few days among those people. These lawmen will quickly give up on us, and then we can go on to Fort Smith."

"This is your land," he said, looking at the range of mountains in the distance.

"Can he jump fences?" she asked.

"Hell, I guess we can try him."

"There's the first one." She whirled Jasper around and, riding sidesaddle, easily swept over the split-rail fence.

Slocum pounded his heels in the big horse's sides and it raced for the fence. He could see the horse would either jump or hit the fence, but the animal easily sailed over it. Belle shouted, and they swept across the great meadow, spooking a few cows. Then Slocum and Belle were gone over another fence to land on a country road.

"I love it," she said. "I bet those damn lawmen don't own a single horse that can steeplechase or fox-hunt. The dumb Union army always had to take down rails to chase the James boys, and they never caught them."

"Do you know people in those mountains?" He didn't completely trust her to tell the truth. She made up so much, and running from the law was serious business in his book. Besides, he wanted someone he could depend on.

"I swear to God, I know lots of these folks. Don't worry."

"They aren't near as likely to shoot you as they are me. Remember that."

"Darling, I am not letting anything happen to you or any part of you." Her grin was wide, and he understood what she meant.

"Oh," she said. "I have a loaf of bread and a small jar of huckleberry jelly. It was about all I could find at Uncle John's. Damn them bastards. I was having fun back there showing you off as Cole."

He nodded and she tore the loaf in two as she rode, and applied half the jar's blue contents to it using the jar bottom for a spreader. Then she rode in close and handed his half to him. "Real fresh. Uncle John makes wonderful bread. Isn't it?"

Slocum's mouth was soon full of sweet jelly and sourdough bread. He nodded. "Real good."

"So now we need supper," she said, looking around at the fields and woods. "We'll find something to eat. Trust me, we will."

They wound their way to the base of the mountains, and took a faint wagon road upward. Late afternoon, they came to a stream that rushed over the rocks in a narrow section wedged between two steep sides. She motioned to him to dismount, and they hitched their horses to some dogwood trees.

"If we had a net and some green walnut hulls in a sack, we could have fish for supper."

"You seen any walnuts?" he asked, opening his war bag.

"Sure. There's some up on that hillside. You have a gunnysack?"

"Right here," he said, drawing it out.

"How are we going to net them?"

"I'm going to tie my sack on two cane sticks and sweep the fish up that you addle."

"You've done this before." She looked put out.

He nodded and grinned. "But it was your idea."

With the skinning knife from his belt, he cut two bamboo stalks stout enough for his purpose, and then sat on the ground while she went after the walnut hulls. The fish scooper was completed when she returned with the hulls in the bottom of the sack. She began unbuttoning her shoes.

When her shoes and hose were finally off, she shed her skirt, exposing her white legs and shapely derriere. She went to the edge of the large water hole and eased herself into the stream.

"Damn, this is cold," she said.

He was at the other end, removing his boots and then his britches. She wobbled a little on some rocks, and he thought she might slip in the stream and go under, but she balanced herself while swishing the sack down into the water.

In a short time, various fishes began to float belly-up around him. First came minnows, which were not worth chasing. Then some small eating-sized bullheads appeared, and next came fat sunfish bigger than his hand, along with some larger green bass to scoop up. He soon had several fish flopping on the bank, and shouted, "We have enough."

She looked up with the water over her knees, and grinned. "We make a good team, don't we?"

"Not bad. Not bad."

She made a face as she looked over at the catch lying in the grass and sand. "I wish I had them cleaned and cooked now."

He walked over to help her out. She tossed up the wet sack with a dozen or so walnut hulls in it, and then let him pull her out and up on the bank. Standing on her toes, she kissed him. "I like fish fried."

"People in jail want out, too, but they ain't going to get out." He clutched the hard half-moons of her butt and pressed her against him. "Tonight, we're having what Texans call barbeque. They do it to everything—beef, sheep, goats, wild burros, deer, and snakes."

"Snakes?"

"I didn't say we were eating them. We're just going to cook the fish like they do everything else."

"Barbeque fish, huh? Never heard of it."

"There's lots of things you haven't heard of."

Her arms around his neck, she rubbed her muff on his bare leg above his knee. "And there's lots that I know how to do, too."

"We're making a fire, cooking fish, and eating them. It'll be dark soon, and then we can play those games you've got on your mind."

"I better put on my skirt then. Folks come by here, they might misunderstand seeing me mooning the world."

He slapped her playfully on the bare ass and laughed. "They might, girl. They just might."

# 4

She made the fire as he dragged in the dry sticks and limbs to feed it. Then, side by side on their hands and knees on a sandbar, they scaled, cleaned, and washed their catch. Using green bamboo sticks, they began to cook the fish over the fire and the hot ashes. Soon, some of the small fish were done and they began to eat them. At first, they were too hot for her, but when she did bite down for the first time, a smile crossed her face. Meanwhile, the last bloody rays of sundown shone through the grove of huge red oaks in front of them.

"I like barbequed fish," she said.

"Hell, see? You're a Texan already."

"No," she said between bites. "I lived there once. It's like you say about California. It is not for me."

As they sat cross-legged on the ground and devoured some of the other cooked fish, he nodded. "All you saw was cotton and corn. I like the cattle and horse operations west of Fort Worth."

"Now, maybe I might like that. You have a place in mind?"

"Me?"

She frowned impatiently at him. "Who else is here?"

"No, I don't have a place. It is way more complicated than that."

"Then you're like Younger and the James boys. The Damnyankees wouldn't give them amnesty. They were fighting a war. What did the Damnyankees expect? Plenty of wrongs were done on both sides. But Younger and the James boys never raped a twelve-year-old girl and laughed about it afterward, did they?"

"You?"

"No. Mary Stockton. She wasn't thirteen yet. They lived on a farm outside of Carthage. We were playing in this old barn. Five of them regulars rode up while it was my turn to swing down, and I was in the loft, getting ready to catch the rope and then fly down on the hay below.

"When I heard her say, 'Who're you?' I knew they was strangers and strangers meant Damnyankees."

She chewed on her lip and shook her head, about to cry. "That leader, he asked where's your papa? Then, from where I crouched out of sight, I could see them through the cracks in the loft floor. They tore off her wash-worn dress. Then they mauled her small breasts, and one of them used his long knife to slice off her flour sack underwear. Mary screamed. So they gagged her.

"Then the big one with the black beard, he dropped his britches and jacked on his rod until it was hard. Then he made them hold her down, legs apart, and he popped her cherry. Oh, it was gruesome. After that, the other four took turns on her until her crotch and inside her legs ran red with blood. They had no—manners—no conscience.

"Later, when I was sure that they were gone, I went and got her mother 'cause Mary was unconscious—from the gag, I guessed. The house was over the hill, so her mother never heard anything nor saw the five men."

"What happened?"

"Mary was so upset about what they did to her, and I guess thinking she could never have a life of her own after that, when she recovered two days later, she hung herself in that barn.

"Those sons a bitches got amnesty. All but one. The one with the black beard. One day, I seen him going in a bar in Fort Smith. So I hired a full-blood to find out where he lived. Elgin Yellow Horse took me to see the man's place and said his name was Taylor. Yellow Horse did all that for the two quarters that I paid him. Then that stupid buck went out with my money and bought a bottle of hooch and got so drunk, he drowned that night in a shallow ditch. I could not help that.

"I hired two more tough ones this time. One was a breed named Eagle. That was not his real name, but he used that name and had a partner named Big Bear. I told them if they would carve out Taylor's balls and bring them to me, I would pay them ten dollars apiece for them.

"They told me that Taylor was tough. That he carried a gun and a knife. I said he came home drunk every night and passed out on a bed. He would be easy to geld in that condition.

"They wanted more money. It was so risky." She made a face in the twilight at Slocum. "I said twenty was all I had. I had more, but that was enough for such a simple job."

"Taylor got drunk on Friday night. They followed him home. I trailed them at a distance. Old Taylor fell down on his porch steps of the shotgun shack where he lived. One under each of his arms, they carried him mumbling and cussing into the bedroom. Eagle lit a small candle lamp. The window was open, so standing outside, I could see and hear what was happening, even with those noisy locusts in the trees buzzing.

"Bear ripped some cloth in strips and they tied his hands to the iron poster bed. Then they jerked off his pants and tied down his feet to each side. Then I saw Bear's knife flash in the candlelight as he held it up.

"Bear said, 'Eagle, you hold his dick up and I'll cut off his bag and all.'

"Guess Eagle didn't want to touch him because he said, 'Let me get a rag. He stinks like shit.'

"Taylor screamed when Bear started carving his sack off. Then he must have fainted because I couldn't hear him anymore. After that, all that I heard was Bear grunting at his work. Then the two blew out the light and slipped out the back door. In the alley, they split up to meet me later down behind Allen's Warehouse on the river. I paid them, and they said if I needed any more studs cut to call on them. They were experts.

"I didn't care if that son of a bitch Taylor died. He never did though, despite Bear's harsh surgery. Later, I saw Taylor around town, and I learned from a gal worked in Molly's Whorehouse that he told the police he never knew who did it. I let his balls dry and was going make me a necklace out of them, but they turned black and stank so bad, I finally threw them away. Wish I had got the other four and did the same to them."

"Whew," Slocum said. "I won't ever let you get mad at me."

"Hmm." She sniffed. "You would have shot him and left him to rot for the buzzards."

"You know—" Then he laughed. "I would have."

She came over and sat in his lap. "The fish were good, but the raccoons will be here tonight to eat the rest we didn't eat."

"Let them eat the rest. I have some jerky for our breakfast."

"So we won't starve?"

"No." Then he kissed her. "You throw down our bedroll and I'll hobble the horses so they can graze some and I'll be back."

"Don't be long. I need you."

He looked hard at her. No telling about her, but for a woman she was horny as he was. He nodded to himself as he went in the starlight to the horses. That was one thing he really liked about her.

# 5

Grandpa Raymond Meyers's sawmill was steam-driven. It shocked Slocum that way up there in the Boston Mountains or White Rock Mountains or wherever they were sat a boiler and a steam engine. The whine of the big blade and the smell of sour sawdust filled the air. Some men were skidding in logs with mules; others were bearing off slabs and stacking the wood boards and ties that the screaming blade was producing.

A white-whiskered man wearing overalls, with a large oil can in his hand, came over, and smiled when he recognized the woman in the sidesaddle.

"Why, Myrabelle Shirley, what are you doing up here?"

She held her finger to her mouth to silence him, and looked things over before sliding off her horse. Straightening her skirt and jacket, she walked over to meet him while leading Jasper.

"Grandpa Meyers, I want you to meet my husband, Cole Younger. But not too loud. We've been dodging lawmen who want him for two days."

"They can't hear much over the damn boiler and that saw blade whining. Nice to meet you, Cole."

Slocum nodded.

"There's Alma," Belle said, and hurried off to hug a woman with graying hair and an apron on over her dress.

"Come on," said Meyers. "We can talk in the office. I don't care who you are, but you damn sure ain't Cole Younger. I met him a few times in the war."

"Slocum's my name. I had a horse go lame several days ago on the main road to Fort Smith. Belle stopped and saved me. When we turned off the main road to a county road, two lawmen from Faulkner County stopped us and asked for sale papers on my mare. I showed them the sale bill and they nodded. I think they thought since I was with Belle, I was probably Younger. She's been using that last name on her trip to Nashville.

"Those two left us acting satisfied. Next day, we went by her Uncle John's place in Coal Hill and we ain't seen any sign of them. But late evening night before last, Ishaid, the black man who works for John, came on the run. He'd learned that those two deputies had sent to Ozark to get a deputy U.S marshal to help them arrest me."

"He's a nice old black man and he looked out for John and his place all through the war and afterwards," said Meyers.

"I know that. I left them the crippled mare and bought the big bay, and as we were leaving, some fella made an attempt to stop us from leaving. Belle ran him plumb over."

"You know that girl can play the piano good as anyone living?" Grandpa Meyers asked him. "Hadn't been for the war, she'd sure've been a society lady."

"I heard her play yesterday. She's very talented."

"By the time she was twelve, she was running messages to troops behind the lines. Wasn't no place for a girl that age to be, but she saved several of their asses from getting ambushed or blown up."

"I bet she did."

"She did, I tell you. But living in them camps with grown men—" He shook his head. "Them women are coming now. I imagine you could eat some dinner."

"Sure could. How's the sawmill business?"

"I've got two thousand cross ties stacked and ready. The government gives the okay to go ahead on them Western railroads, they could be worth two bucks apiece. Or if they stall around much, they could be worth two bits. My boys took a week off and we put in everyone's crops, used my mules and teams to get the job done. We have a good growing season, they'll have food to eat. They ain't had a payday since last December. They're with me and they won't mention you two to anyone."

"Good."

"Those women get in, I have an idea that might help you two."

"Thanks, we can use one."

"Well," Belle said, coming in the doorway. "You going to buy his sawmill?"

"We've been talking money and terms," said Slocum.

"He done told me about the deputies on your backside," said Meyers. "Alma and I have a nice cabin hid out on Blackburn Creek. We use it to picnic sometimes just to be alone."

"Oh, we've stayed over there several days at a time," Alma said. "No road in there, only a trail. Old man sold it to Raymond a couple years ago before he died. He wanted the money to buy a headstone, so we call it Marker Cabin. He only lived about a year and half longer and passed away, but he had a large stone on his grave when they put him under it."

"Is it hard to find?" Slocum asked.

"No, I can draw you a map," Raymond said. "We can outfit you with enough supplies and you two can stay up there for ten days or so, then ride on. They won't find you up there and there's plenty of feed for your horses. Lots of bluestem grass in the bottoms."

"What do you think?" Slocum asked Belle.

"Cool our heels a few days up there will be fine with me."

Their heels might be cool up there, but their other parts

were liable to be real sore. They could even rename it Honeymoon Cabin when they got through.

"You sit right here," Alma said, pulling out the head chair at the dining table for Slocum.

"But that's Raymond's seat, I'd bet."

"I don't care. I want to tell my grandkids that Cole Younger sat in the head chair in my dining room."

Raymond winked at him to go ahead. Boy, was she in for a razzing when they rode out and he told her the truth—whether he really would or not, Slocum was uncertain.

"I want to tell you about that cabin's location," said Raymond. "Blackburn Creek flows into Lee's Creek and following it, you can reach the old military road by going down that drainage, then ride into Van Buren on that road."

"Good thing to know." Slocum passed the bowl of shelled peas to Belle.

"What did I tell you?" Belle said, and elbowed him.

He nodded. She'd done well so far. Knowing the underground railroad for Rebs was a good way to survive. When Alma passed the meat platter, he admired the large slabs of ham she had fried for their lunch.

"Aw, take two pieces," Alma said. "A big fellar like you will need his energy."

He smiled and obeyed her.

"There's plenty more where that came from."

They had fried sugar-cured ham, peas, mashed potatoes, and plenty of thick flour gravy, along with huge fresh hot biscuits and real butter. Slocum had not had a meal this good in months.

"Sure fine food, ma'am."

"Oh, Mr. Younger, it is so nice to have you at my table. I swear, them church ladies will cry when they find out."

"Can't tell them a thing for weeks," Raymond said. "I don't want Colt Broom hearing he's around here until they are plumb out of the country."

"Who's Colt Broom?" Slocum asked, looking up from his food for an answer.

"A bounty hunter who lives over on the Middle Fork of the White River. A ruthless man," Raymond said.

"Butcher," Alma added. "He murdered my brother Tad. Claimed he was a spy and them Yanks paid him fifty dollars for his head in a tow sack."

"What's he look like, Raymond?" Slocum asked in case they met up with him.

"Red whiskers, though his hair is brown. Stands over six and a half feet tall. Big as any bear I ever saw."

"He ever come up here?"

Raymond nodded. "He wears a top hat or a red handkerchief tied over his brown hair. I upset him last time he came across the mountain to here. Right off, he went to ordering my men around like he was some kinda general. I've got a Remington Sharp Shooter rifle with a scope I bought off a soldier coming home. I shot the hat off Broom's head and then I told him to get in the saddle and ride, 'cause I was lowering my next shot four inches. He ain't been back since." Raymond laughed.

"He know you own that place over there?" Slocum asked.

"Sure, but he likes the easy places to raid."

"I'll watch for him." Slocum had heard of the likes of Colt Broom all over the South.

"Do that. He ain't nice."

"Alma, this is a terrific meal," Slocum said, taking seconds on his plate.

She beamed, looking about halfway embarrassed by his words. "Ain't often we get us a real important guest up here. Oh, this is just usual dinner."

After lunch, Raymond and Alma fixed them enough food for an army in two panniers, and threw in a half-draft, half-saddle-horse cross to pack it up to the cabin. Slocum offered to buy the horse, but Raymond would have nothing to do with his money.

"You take good care of Myrabelle and that'll be payment enough."

"I promise I'll do that."

Then Raymond drew him a map in the dirt. "After you pass over this mountain here, draw up and wait a few hours. Then you'll know if they're tracking you."

"Good idea."

"I ain't saying anyone here would spill the beans, but you can't tell who you rode by coming up here that might not have let his shirttail hit his ass before running and telling someone you two rode by there."

Slocum nodded. He understood about those kind.

When the horses and pack animal were ready, he gave Belle a boost into her sidesaddle and they were ready to take leave of the noisy sawmill. Belle thanked them again and they rode west.

There were lots of ties stacked around ready to be hauled out for the emerging railroads. Slocum hoped Raymond got two dollars apiece for them—but who knows. They hit the mountain road headed west, the smell of wood smoke in the air. Clearings with dogtrot log cabins lined the road. There were also rough-hewed square cabins, with crops coming up in the fields behind split-rail fences used to keep the free-range livestock like hogs, cattle, and even draft animals out.

Several women sat on porch rockers, smoked corncob pipes, and waved. Young children ran out to the road to look with curious eyes at the fancy lady riding sidesaddle and the Texas man under the cowboy hat.

A freckled-faced boy ran alongside them. "You going back to Texas, mister?"

"I reckon so," Slocum said, smiling down at the barefoot youth.

"Take me with you." He blinked, looking up in the mid-afternoon sun at Slocum.

"Why, your ma needs you, son."

"Naw, she don't. She's got my stepdad and I hate him."

"I'm sorry. We're traveling light. We ain't got any room for a boy."

"Aw, mister, I'd be your slave to get to go to Texas."

"Sorry."

The boy dropped back and the last time Slocum saw him, stood shaking his head in disgust.

"I'm surprised you did not take him with you," Belle said as they dropped off the mountaintop and into the steep woods that lined the downhill portion of the road.

"Guess you know I was tempted. But you can't just take along every boy that runs out and begs you to."

She pursed her lips and shook her head. "I think derelicts and outlaws are attracted to you like a magnet."

"Which one are you?"

She wrinkled her nose at him as they rode side by side in an easy trot. "Damned if I know—outlaw?"

They came to the headwaters of the West Fork River with a pool big enough to bathe in, and made camp in the grassy bottoms at the base of the hill. He gathered Belle firewood to cook with, then unsaddled and hobbled their horses while she made supper in the pots Alma had sent along.

Coffee was ready when he sat down in the sundown light that gilded everything in the valley before it settled down behind the western horizon. A farmer with two wagons had camped across the stream, and his children soon went swimming naked in the pool that Belle had picked out to use later herself.

She scowled in the firelight. "Those little bastards took my water hole. Why, for two cents, I would go over there and shoot their asses off."

"Why be mad at them? They've been riding in those wagons all day. They deserved that break." He caught her and hugged her. "Land's sake, you can get mad like snapping a torpedo-head match aflame."

He could feel the tremors still going through her body as they settled back on the ground on top of the blanket behind some bushes. She turned and began kissing him with a wild abandon that matched her earlier anger. He undid the ties on her skirt, and soon his flat hand was moving over her smooth skin downward until his fingers raked through the coarse pubic hair. She widened her knees for his entry, and he began to slowly probe her.

Her breathing quickened with his finger inside her, and she turned toward his hand. His actions increased and she tore her mouth from his to breathe.

"Dear God, you are the—horniest man I have ever met. Oh, I love it. Love it . . ."

In seconds, they were shedding clothing, and she shook her head in mild defeat as she cleared her legs of her skirt. "We can do it with my damn shoes on. I ain't taking the time now."

He agreed. Soon they were coupled together and going for the treasure that lay at the end of their hard-pounding tryst. His throbbing hard erection was plunging into her wild contractions. Air became a precious commodity, and his head felt light as a cloud when at last, with a pounding heart, he came hard inside her. *Belle Younger, you are a real crazy wild darling witch.*

# 6

Dawn came in a purple light in the east. They were saddled and the packhorse was loaded before the peach light appeared above the forest. On the dirt road, as the horses' hooves churned up a skim of dust, they trotted westbound. A few doves called, and crows added to the chorus as they dived down to check for something to eat and strode around in the roadway like black emperors from one pile of horse apples to the next in search of some undigested grain.

More farms and fields appeared. Milk cows bawled at them. A calf cried, too, separated from its momma. The rasping honking of a mule or two could be heard. A man who looked like a doctor drove by in a buggy with a nod. Chickens were scratching in the road, and scattered before the horses. A cocky-acting red rooster with his wings dropped down went scooting around them like he might attack one of the horses. Slocum laughed at his antics.

"How far are we from the cabin?" Belle asked.

"Oh, we should make it by afternoon. But—" He twisted in the saddle to be certain that no one was around. "Raymond suggested when we got over the next range that we hold up in the woods for a while and see if we have drawn any company."

"Oh." She nodded, riding stirrup to stirrup beside him.

"Strangers draw conversation, and we don't want to be the ones that lead them to the cabin."

She nodded. "This place sounds like it is going to be a Garden of Eden."

He looked over at her and grinned. "You going to be Eve?"

"I may be. But am I keeping you from getting a job on a cattle drive this year?"

"There will always be cattle drives, I figure. Might not always be a Belle Younger."

"Might be someone a damn sight prettier."

"I haven't seen one lately, or better looking."

"Why, I bet you tell all the women you seduce that."

"The road forks up ahead. There's a store there. I'm going to let them believe we're going to Texas via Fort Smith and ask at the store where we can catch the Butterfield Road."

Her dark eyes narrowed and she nodded. "Will that throw them off?"

"I hope so. That's my plan."

Later, he came out of the cabin that had been turned into a store. A man wearing a white shirt and galluses got up from the checkers game he was having with two farmers in homemade clothing.

"Howdy, stranger, you passing through our community today?"

Slocum, ready to mount up, nodded. "Headed for Fort Worth. The lady inside told us this road will lead us to the Military Road and Fort Smith."

The man scratched the white thatch of short hair on his head, and then used his hand to indicate the direction west. "It will if you follow it to where Lee's Crick crosses that road. Ain't hard to find either."

Slocum bounced off his toe and swung in the saddle. "Thanks, we'll find it."

"Fine horse you're a-riding,"

"He'll do all right. Have a nice day, sir. Let's go," Slocum said to Belle.

"I didn't catch your name, sir."

"I didn't give it, did I?"

"No, sir."

"Next time, I'll have more time and tell you." He put heels to his horse and left.

"When will that be?" the white-shirted man shouted after him.

"Can't say." Belle was already five lengths ahead of him going up the steep S-shaped road that led to a new horizon above them. He left the small settlement with his horse cat-hopping up the steep mountain face on a road that no doubt made log haulers and others in conveyances cringe in fear when descending.

In a half mile, the world flattened out and they were bound southwesterly through woods and more farmland. When they came to the fork, he pointed right and nodded, looking back. This was close to where Raymond wanted them to stop and observe their back trail for a while.

They reached the trail that Raymond had described, and Slocum sent her ahead leading his horse along with the packhorse as he wiped out their tracks with some brush.

When the prints were well enough covered, he hurried to catch up with her. They rode on to a small clearing where several large white oak trees had been sawed down and the blocks cut out with crosscuts and split into barrel staves, except for a few too knotty to split. Slocum and Belle went to the far side of the clearing and hid the horses, then came back and waited.

Eating some jerky and seated on the ground, they whiled away several hours, but no pursuit showed up. Satisfied, they caught their horses and rode off in the deep canyon.

Finally, they were in the bottoms. He could hear the rushing water when he spotted the cabin. She nodded at the sight. The knee-high meadows of bluestem ran down beside the sparkling creek, all walled in by sheer bluffs of lime and sandstone.

"It does look like the Garden of Eden," she said.

He glanced up at the forested mountains above the cliffs that hemmed them in. "Yes, it might be just that place."

He felt envious that Raymond owned such a great hide-away, with a nice stream of water and tall grass meadows. A good place to hide with the panniers full of food until the news of Cole Younger's appearance in western Arkansas died down. Besides that, he had Belle to share this place with him.

Their horses splashed water crossing the small stream, and they rode up to the front door. Slocum looked around to survey things, then dismounted. She was already inside the door as he hitched his horse to the rack out in front.

She about collided with him in the doorway. "It is a wonderful place."

He surveyed the room and the iron poster bed. How did they ever get that down here? Oh, well, where there was a will, there was a way. He hugged and kissed her and then swept off his hat.

"We get unpacked and the horses hobbled, we'll have to test that bed."

She pushed the hair back from his forehead as she looked up at him. "On the floor. In a bed. Darling, I can use you any of those places that you want me."

He squeezed her tight and kissed her again. It was heady business, him and this hot-bloodied Southern Belle alone in paradise. But first, he had to unload and hobble the horses—damn, it was going to be hard to leave her to do that. But he did.

Late afternoon, he swung back and forth in a large rocker, watching her scurry about as she cooked in the stone fireplace. Some good stone mason had built it and, like other things in the cabin, it was not a patch-and-run effort. There were even swinging iron holders that allowed Belle to move her pots over the heat or draw them to the edge to keep warm.

Split chinkapin wood in the fire sent off small explosions that cracked and then burst like fireworks. What had his grandfather said? "Make my coffin from chinkapin boards, boys, so I go cracking and popping through hell when I get there." Of course, when the time came, his grandmother would never hear about doing that. Slocum smiled, remembering those words as he rocked back and forth and watched her crouched at the fireplace working on supper.

"Oh, I have some coffee," she said, noticing him.

"Good, I can drink some. I'll find a cup."

"Stay seated. I have some here."

"That's not hard. Sitting here, I mean, while you work."

She shook her head at the insinuation about "hard." "How did I ever find you? Oh, that mare and her limp. Now, was that real or only a trick to get me to stop?"

"Belle, if I'd known you were coming and would stop, I'd've made her limp."

They both laughed.

Squatted down, she looked around. "I wish I'd known about this cabin before. I'd a came here and hid out."

"There was an old man lived here then, and I suspect he was the craftsman who built this place."

"He wanted a tombstone for his grave, didn't he?"

"That's the story Raymond told."

"Well, I simply love it." She rose and brought Slocum a cup of steaming coffee.

The tin cup was hot, and he slipped off his kerchief and used it to hold the cup.

"What's cattle driving like?" she asked.

"Hot, dusty, and dangerous. Those longhorns are close to being deer and stampede over nothing. The work is hell. You ride herd all day and half the night. At times, your bedding never gets dry. You eat dust or freeze in the rain and hail."

"I guess the money is why they do it?"

"Money motivates most men."

"That and women—" She smiled smugly back at him while on her haunches and pulling a hinged hanging pot out to stir it with a wooden spoon. "There is sure not any money in hauling my fanny around. So it must be the latter that you are interested in."

"I am. I am."

She about fell over laughing at his reply. With the finger-tips of one hand touching the polished floor to keep her in position, she regained her balance. "Your supper is ready."

Later, in bed with him on top of her, he heard the brazen howl of a red wolf and paused.

"A wolf, isn't it?" she asked.

He nodded in the cabin's cozy darkness, and then he shoved his dick deep inside her. Must be a big leader of a pack. He could visualize the rusty-colored male loping along, his red tongue hanging out and his coal black eyes looking hard for a possible meal. Then he turned his attention back to her, thrusting in and out of her contracting ring of fire until she cried out and fainted.

"Oh," she moaned. "What was that?"

"You talking about the wolf or you fainting?"

Out of breath, she blinked her watery eyes. "I never did that before. I never fainted, not in bed or anywhere else." She gulped for more air. "Damn you. Slocum, I am so dizzy I think I could fall off this bed."

"No, you can't. I am still plugged in."

She swept the hair from her face and shook her head. "I'm glad you like women more than money."

They both laughed, and he shoved his dick into her deeper again.

# 7

In the bright morning sun, Slocum was using both hands on the ax handle to split wood. He brought the ax over his head and then down to split off the next piece of stove wood. From the corner of his eye, he saw his horse and Jasper, across the creek, throw up their heads from grazing and stare in the direction of the trail. Someone or something was coming.

He sunk the ax in the chopping block and rushed for the cabin to warn Belle. He burst in the doorway. "Get your gun. We've got company coming."

From the ladder-back chair, he swept up his gun belt, unbuckled it, and strapped it on his waist. A rifle would be a good thing to have at that moment. Their cap-and-ball pistols were close-range weapons. But they didn't have a rifle. Maybe the intruder had a short-range weapon, too. If he was more than a lost soul, Slocum could hope that was all he had for armaments.

She came over with her revolver on her waist and stood behind him at the doorway, where he studied the mountain.

"I wonder who it is," she said.

Slocum shook his head. "He's either lost or is looking for us."

48

Then three armed riders appeared coming off the mountain. Two rode mules, the third one a stout gray mare. The first two were the Faulkner County deputies. The third man looked more official.

"It's them," she said.

Slocum nodded. "We aren't having a shoot-out with the law. I'm not Cole Younger."

"Those no-good sons a bitches. How did they ever find us down here?" She swore under her breath. "What do we do?"

"Listen to what they have to say."

"But they may arrest you."

"There's worse things than that. I'm not Cole Younger and they'll find that out."

"But what if they kill you?"

"We'll take it one step at a time. Go easy and don't lose your temper. It won't help."

"I will try."

When the three rode out of the creek, Slocum stepped out of the cabin. "Hold it up right there and state your business."

"I'm Myron Hamby, a deputy U.S. marshal," said the first man. "Those two are Carr and Sims. Are you Cole Younger?" The man was heavyset and his sideburns were white. He looked all business.

"No, sir. I am not Cole Younger. My name is Slocum. John Slocum. I have never been Cole Younger."

Hamby turned and talked softly to the two deputies. Then he cleared his throat and checked his gray mare before he spit tobacco off to the side. "These two gentlemen disagree."

"If they had a reward poster, they'd know that Cole Younger has blond hair. Mine is dark brown. He's a much broader-built man than I am and has blue eyes."

Hamby gripped his saddle horn and shook his head in dismay. "You know Cole Younger then?"

"I have met him on a few occasions. Do you or those men with you have a poster describing Younger?"

"Unfortunately, no."

"Then I assume that your business here is completed?" Slocum asked.

"One of my jobs is arresting owners of untaxed stills."

"We don't have a still here," Slocum said.

"Mind if we look around?"

"You'd need a search warrant to do that, wouldn't you, by the law?"

Hamby nodded. "I asked for your permission."

"Permission denied." Slocum had no idea what they knew or what he didn't know about this place. Up the holler, there could be a setup he knew nothing about.

"Only a man who had something to hide would refuse to allow us to look."

"Get your warrant and come back. This is the United States of America."

Belle stepped outside and Hamby removed his hat. "Good day, ma'am."

Arms folded over her breasts, she didn't bother to do more than nod at his greeting.

"First, those two stopped us over a horse that he'd bought and paid for," she said. "Now, you ride clear up here to implicate us in a whiskey still that, if it is here, is certainly not ours."

"Sorry, ma'am, but that's my job."

"Well, then, get out of here and go get your warrant."

"Ma'am, I will do that." Hamby started to turn his horse to leave.

"Good riddance, and take those other two yahoos with you."

"Yes, ma'am."

Belle was livid with anger, muttering under her breath about those worthless no-account lawmen. Slocum watched them talking together as they crossed the knee-deep creek. They were making plans no doubt. At that moment, he wished he was a mouse in Hamby's pocket.

"What will we do?" she asked from beside him.

"Wait till they're gone," he said under his breath.

"Those no-account sonsabitches are going to spoil Eden for us, ain't they?"

"It looks that way to me."

She stamped her foot on the ground. "Bastards. For two cents, I'd fill them full of lead."

"That's what I didn't want. Raymond said this stream led to Lee's Creek, and that stream led to Military Road. We can be in Fort Smith in a few days and I'll be on my way to Fort Worth."

"You leaving me?"

He hugged her. "What would you do on a cattle drive?"

"A lot of damn things."

"We can talk about that later. I figure Hamby left one of those deputies, maybe two, up there on the mountain to guard the trail out of here. Tonight, if we can sneak up on them and take their mules, they won't get back to civilization very fast on foot. After we get their mules, we'll have the packhorse loaded and get out of here going down the creek."

"That sounds good. Why wouldn't you let them search the place?"

"I'm not sure they wouldn't find an old still around here and hang that charge on us."

"Good thinking. What are we going to do next?"

He whispered in her ear. "Let's us go use that bed. They're gone for now and we may not get another chance before we have to ride out."

"Whew, I am not over the last time." Then, with the flat of her hands, she drove him toward the doorway. "You know, you make me dizzy."

"Good."

Slocum took a final look at the mountain. Their own horses were grazing and not paying any attention to anything around them, so the lawmen might have left for the time being. Once inside, he barred the door and then hung his gun belt close to the bed.

Seated in the middle of the bed, with her knees tucked

under her chin, Belle was busy unhooking her shoes. "I may start wearing cowboy boots, huh?"

Undressed and hanging his pants up, he smiled back at her. "Depends how fast you want to do something."

"Oh, I could be so mad. Those dumb lawmen busting in here and making us leave this place. Just when I'm— enjoying you so much."

He knelt on the bed, and she let her legs drop so he could unbutton her blouse. Soon, he was fondling her breasts from behind her, until she finally raised her head and shook it. "Let me undo this last shoe and you can screw me until sundown."

"Promise?"

"Oh, do I ever." Feverishly, she fought the last hooks open and then tossed the shoe on the floor. Raising up, she untied the skirt and pushed it off her snowy legs.

"You drive me crazy. You know that?"

He slipped onto the bed beside her, and his hand ran over her pubic mound. Excitement tingled all over his bare skin—her supple body intoxicated him and had become real habit forming.

After nightfall, they started up the mountain on foot to check out if any of the lawmen were standing guard. Being quiet as they could be, they slipped though the hardwood forest with its deep shadows and the sour smell of decaying leaf litter strong in the still air.

Slocum heard a mule cough, and reached out to stop her.

"They aren't far away," he said in her ear. "I don't want them shot."

She nodded. They moved slower from there on, circling west to come in behind them. Soon the small campfire's light was obvious, and Slocum could see one of the deputies was sitting up.

They worked closer, tree by tree. Until he nodded at her. *Close enough.* He drew his .44 and stepped out.

"Hands high!"

The two started to scramble, but his well-placed shot in their fire sent sparks flying and both men froze on their hands and knees. Belle came out to join him, and began to use her riding quirt on Carr, who was still on his hands and knees.

"You no-account sneaking sumbitch!" she screamed.

Slocum rushed over and jerked her back by the arm. "They gave up. Quit it, damnit."

Wild-eyed in the firelight, she tried to dart around Slocum to get at Carr. "I'm going to beat them senseless. Coming up here and rooting us out of our Eden—"

"We have them, Belle," he said through his teeth, tightening his grip on her forearm.

She managed to get close enough to kick Carr in the shoulder. "There, take that, you stupid sonabitch."

Tired of her tantrums, Slocum forced her down on the ground. Still mad, she sat shaking, folded her arms, and then pouted.

"Where did Hamby go?" he asked, taking the deputies' sidearms.

"To get a search warrant," Carr said.

"Did he figure there is a still down there somewhere that he can blame on me?"

"He believed enough in it to ride clear to Van Buren for a warrant."

"Save him the time when he returns. There ain't one down there."

"He will be pissed when he get back."

"Find me their handcuffs," Slocum said to Belle, and turned back to his prisoners. "We could have shot you. Remember that the next time. We will shoot to kill if we see you again."

Both men nodded, and Belle returned with the cuffs. "Where do you want them?"

"On the ground. Carr, get out your key and unlock them."

"What are you planning on doing to us?" Carr asked, handing over the key ring.

"Hanging your hatchet ass from some tree," Belle said, still spitting-fire mad.

"Both on your feet. Sims, give me your keys."

The deputy frowned at him. "What in the hell for?"

"'Cause he told you to!" Belle snapped.

Slocum held out his hand for the keys. She threw some more sticks on the fire to build it up. He took the keys from Sims.

Then he chained the two deputies around a big oak with their own handcuffs. They were locked tight enough that they'd have to stand up until Hamby returned. That would take away some of the hurry to get on his and Belle's trail.

"I ever get you in my gun sights, I'll kill both of you," Sims shouted as Slocum and Belle saddled the two men's mules.

"Yeah, sure," Belle said, drawing up the latigos on her mule's cinch. "You had to go get Hamby to even try to arrest us. You two are big, bad lawmen."

Slocum shook his head at her when he caught her looking his way. No need to gouge them too deep. They wouldn't forget Slocum and Belle, that was certain.

Under the starlight, Slocum and Belle rode off down the trail. Slocum never really liked the short-coupled jerky gait of a mule, even when walking one, but it sure beat walking. In the bottom, he unsaddled the mules and hobbled them so they didn't follow him and Belle. He hid the deputies' saddles on the rafters in a small shed, and then cut the headstalls apart.

Then he joined her. She was already sitting on her horse and holding the reins and lead to the other two horses. He swung up on his horse, and under the stars they set out down Blackburn Creek as Raymond had suggested.

The trail proved to be faint. Belle became tangled in possum grapevines that she couldn't duck riding sidesaddle. Slocum rushed back to help her, and then they rode on. When they reached the next creek fork a few hours later, a wagon road appeared and they followed it westward along

Blackburn Creek. There were no more incidents, and when the sky began to glow pink over their shoulders, they reached Lee's Creek.

The larger stream rushed over the rocks and boulders, and the crossing was knee-deep on the horses. On the far bank, Slocum dismounted and looked around. An abandoned farm sat back in a meadow filled with weeds. It would do for their purposes.

"Let's go up there and sleep awhile," he said, and remounted.

She agreed. In back of the small house, there was a trap grown up in grass and bushes that would hold their horses and keep them out of sight from the road. He left them saddled—in case he and Belle needed to flee at a moment's notice.

"We can chew on some crackers and dry cheese, sleep a few hours, and then ride on." He stood in the doorway of the hewed-log building. The floor was dirt. He rolled out the bedroll on the part of the floor with no debris.

She nodded numbly. "I'm not hungry."

He undid his gun belt, placing it near where his head would be. Seated, she took her holster set off, too, and then fell back on the roll. They snuggled in each other's arms and fell asleep.

When he awoke, he heard a wagon going by down on the road—the jog trot of big unshod horses, harness chains ringing, and the crush of sandstone under iron wheel rims.

"What is it?" she hissed.

"Wagon going past."

"Oh." She lay back down on her folded hands and closed her eyes.

"We better get on our way. I suspect it's past noon."

"You, sir, are a slave driver." She sat up and braced herself on one hand.

"I hate jails. Did I tell you?"

She nodded. In a few minutes, they were moving again, riding southwesterly on the wagon road. With hard strokes, she brushed her long hair as she rode sidesaddle. At tangles, she grimaced, pulling the brush through them.

Some range hogs rushed out of the willows and cane to scurry across the road. Their woofing and grunts made Jasper spook sideways, and it about upset Belle, but she kept her seat. Then, with her horse under control, she threatened the disappeared shoats with her hairbrush and shouted some choice unladylike words after them.

That evening they reached Union Town, and Slocum never stopped. In the twilight, he knew anyone tracking them could ask if a woman and a man had ridden through there. Belle in the sidesaddle made them too obvious even at night. They reached Van Buren late in the night, and left their horses at Pritchard's Livery. Belle swore they could trust Pritchard.

Then, after a meal in a small café where they were the only customers, she led him down the street and up a set of stairs on the side of a brick building. A sleepy-eyed black girl in her teens answered the door, clutching a robe to her body with one hand and a candle holder in the other.

"Why, Miss Belle, what 'cha doing here at dis time of the night?"

"Hush, darling. Me and—we need a room for the night." She indicated Slocum.

"You's can have number five."

"Good, I'll settle with Hattie in the morning."

"No problem," the girl said, leading them to room five with her lamp making a ring of light on the hallway floor and her dark bare feet.

"I done changed the sheets in here." She opened the door and pushed it back to let them inside.

Slocum lit a lamp and nodded thanks.

Belle herded the girl out, thanking her, and then shut the door.

"Whew," she said, and rested her butt against it. "You sure can cover lots of ground in a long day."

He was toeing off his boots. "I told you I hate jails. This place a whorehouse?"

She laughed and pushed herself upright. "It is not your first one either, sir. Let's go to bed. I am totally exhausted."

He agreed, looking out the window at the dark street. They'd be in Fort Smith the next day. Then he'd head south on the Texas Road for Fort Worth. It was still early enough that there would be a cattle drive there for him to take to Kansas.

He stretched his arms over his head and yawned. Then he felt her hug him from behind and press her body against his back. "Well, cowboy, what next?"

A good question.

# 8

Fort Smith bustled with traffic. Steam whistles hooted from the riverboats, people were shouting, and horse, dray, and carriage traffic filled Garrison Avenue. Bicycles pedaled through the sidewalk traffic. Pedestrians wore bib overalls, canvas pants, or rags. There were men in business suits and small hats, and Mexican drovers with dusty wide straw sombreros. Sailors from the river traffic wore their flat caps, and lots of Indians and breeds sat around smugly wrapped in blankets despite the growing heat.

"I love this place," Belle said as they rode through the congestion of the street and around the blacks with their wheelbarrows, brooms, and shovels picking up the horse apples.

He nodded, keeping a sharp eye out in case anyone challenged them. "You going to stay here?" he asked.

"Why? You don't want me?"

He shook his head. "It might be easier than going to Texas."

"You're going down there to find a herd of cattle and drive them to Kansas?"

"I intend to do that."

"Well, unless you are mad at me or tired of me, I am going along."

That's what he'd thought deep in his heart. She'd want to go. But trail drives and women? He wasn't certain they went together. Besides, she'd soon grow weary of it and pull out. "Ain't no way I'm tired of you."

"Good. When do we go to Fort Worth?" she asked.

With his fingertips, he rubbed a spot on his forehead under his hat brim. When? "Soon."

"Good. I need to collect a little money owed me."

Curious as he was about who owed her money and for what, he simply nodded. Might be better not to ask—since she still had not explained to him how she knew so much about Hattie's place in Van Buren.

They stabled their horses at Ferguson's Livery and took a room on her suggestion at Mrs. Kline's boardinghouse. It was late afternoon when they parted in front of the boardinghouse and he went to find a poker game in some saloon on Garrison. She was off to collect "some money."

His poker in Hennesey's Saloon on Garrison with a few tinhorns, a boat captain, and a mule buyer proved profitable enough. He knew he had won somewhere around seventy-five dollars when he folded to go find Belle for supper around eight that night. In the boardinghouse room, he discovered her napping. She sat up sleepy-eyed, wearing a white gown.

"Are you hungry?" he asked.

She stretched like a dreamy mountain lion and smiled. "For you?"

"I had food in mind."

"Yes, I could eat. I'll dress. Did you win at gambling?" She fought the gown off over her head and stood naked in the bloodred light of sundown that shone in their open window.

"Seventy-two dollars."

She raised her eyebrows and smiled. "Not bad."

"Did you collect your money?" he asked.

"A portion of it." She turned the corner of her lip up in disgust. "I staked a man to some money six months ago. He promised to pay me back in a short while, but has been avoiding me ever since. Guess I am a sorry judge of men. So he paid me half of what he owed me today. Then, if you can imagine, he expected me to climb into bed with him for his generosity."

She shook her head, busy brushing her hair in long strokes that made her breasts shake. "If he thought for one moment I'd do that with him, he was crazy."

Slocum laughed.

Brandishing the brush in her hand to threaten him, she said, "It is not funny."

He crossed the room and hugged her. "You get so furious at times. One of these days, you'll have a stroke over it."

"What did you expect me to do?"

"Oh, don't get mad because he asked." Then he kissed her, and she dropped the brush and threw her arms around his neck.

"Damn you, Slocum. I wanted to make you jealous."

Gently, he fondled her left breast and nibbled on her neck. She looked to the tin ceiling for help. "Oh, hell, go ahead and dump me on the bed. I can see we are not going out to eat for a while."

Slocum laughed and did as she told him.

An hour later, they were seated in Ho Chang's Chinese restaurant, in the basement under Watson's Saloon. The place was frequented by the wealthy, and also some of the town's less fortunate residents. No one that he knew was in there, or at least, no one that he recognized in the dim candlelight.

She smirked, and then leaned over to whisper, "See that fat old man at that back table? His name's Ferd Williams the Third, and that little slut with him is Carolyn, his latest mistress."

"What does Williams do?"

"Screw her, I guess. If he can."

"No, what is his source of money?"

"Oh, he owns several buildings downtown and the Cattleman's Bank."

A waiter delivered their plates heaping with food as Slocum wondered about Williams and his affair. The smell of cooked beef and soy sauce filled the air. His empty stomach complained, and he couldn't clearly recall his last real meal.

They both ate like half-starved wolves, and when they finished, collapsed in their chairs.

"Wonderful," she sighed.

He watched Williams and his mistress leaving the restaurant. "Where's she from?"

"St. Louis, I think. She first came here, she worked at Meagan's house. But she wasn't going to stay there long. Some tinhorn bailed her out of there. She still owed Meagan for her transportation to get down here. Once outside of Meagan's, she quickly left the gambler and wormed her way into Williams's protection and money pile."

"A girl's got to do what she can," Slocum said.

"Yes, that is why I want to go on your cattle drive."

He nodded. "We'll see. I don't have one yet."

"Oh, you will get one." She yawned and covered her mouth with her hand.

"That reminds me. One more night here and I'm going south."

"So am I."

"Good, that's settled."

She reached over and squeezed his hand. "You do want me along, don't you?"

He winked. "Yes, but—"

"I know. I know. It is dangerous and boring."

"Let's go find that bed. We're both tired to the bone."


A day later, they used the steam-driven ferry to cross the Arkansas River before daylight, and then climbed the road of ties laid in the sandy bank. On their right was a "shanty town" where all the outcasts of society—derelicts, drunks, and breed Indians with their skinny dogs—lived in crate shacks, ragged canvas tents, and dugouts.

They soon were racing the sun westward. His decision to take the Texas Road south rather than the old Butterfield Road was based on there being less law enforcement stationed in the Indian Territory than in Arkansas. Hamby was bound to swear out a warrant for him, which would be less likely to be served in the Indian Territory.

They crossed the Canadian on a hand-powered ferry late that day. Belle wanted to visit some people that she knew, and they arrived at their house long after sundown.

"These people know Cole, so you go back to being Slocum, all right?" she asked him before they dismounted.

"Sure."

"You home, Nicolas?" she shouted above the hound dogs barking in the front yard.

A bare-chested man with a shotgun answered the door. "That you, Belle?"

"It is not your last mother-in-law."

"Thank Gawd for that! Get down and who's with you?"

"He is a friend of mine. Slocum is his name."

Nicolas set the shotgun down back inside the door. "Any friend of yours, Belle, is a friend of mine. Get down, stranger—I mean Slocum."

"Much obliged," Slocum said, surrounded by hounds that wanted to sniff him out.

"Where did you hail from?"

"Lately? Fort Smith."

"Hell, no one lives there. They just visit that place."

"That's about the truth," Belle said, sliding off her horse into Slocum's arms. "They've got the business, though. Saloons are full and there's even lines, they say, at the parlor houses."

"Whew. We can put them horses up later. Come in. Sally, Sally, get up. We've got us company."

"Who?"

"Belle Younger and a fellar."

"Why, for land's sake. Is she really here, Nick?"

"She is unless I went blind drinking Hawkin's shine."

"Belle," the shorter woman screamed, and rushed into the shadowy kitchen to hug her. They danced around the room a little, and then hugged each other again.

"They're like two sisters," Nick explained to Slocum. "Go plumb crazy every time they get reunited. Let's put up your stock. They'll settle down in a few minutes and make us some food."

Nick combed his woolly hair back with his fingers. "I swear, they sure get all heated up when they find each other."

Slocum nodded, and followed the man out into the starlight. When the horses were unsaddled and the panniers stored so no coon or varmint could tear into them, Nick found a Mason jar hidden in the hay and unscrewed the top. "Handy for canning, but damn sure good for keeping shine in."

He handed the jar to Slocum, who took a good sip and handed the jar back, wiping his face on his sleeve. The liquor went down smooth and warmed his ears. It wasn't that fiery hot. In fact, it was some of the best sipping whiskey he'd had since before the war at home.

"The man made that knows his business," Slocum said.

Nick agreed, and handed him back the jar.

"No, thanks, I've had enough for now. That could set a man back on his ass pretty fast."

"Or out cold. That's powerful stuff all right." Nick screwed on the lid and hid the jar back in the hay. "Let's go see about some grub."

"You farm down here?" Slocum asked,

"Naw, I've got a sharecropper does that."

The women finally settled down and cooked a meal for Belle and Slocum. Afterward, Nick and Slocum sat out on the porch and listened to the tree frogs croak and talked about the times while the women cleaned up the dishes.

"Where you headed next?" Nick asked.

"Fort Worth. I'd like to catch a cattle drive going north."

"They say there's been plenty of them big herds going north this spring way out west of here."

"I've been hurrying to get down there." Slocum snickered. "Well, I been aiming to go there anyway."

"Ah, that Belle Younger is quite a distraction."

In the shadowy light coming on the porch, he could see a knowing look on Nick's face. "Yes, quite."

Slocum and Belle left early the next morning. That day they ate a sausage sandwich made by a crossroads storekeeper at noontime, and took another along to eat later for supper. They slept under an oak tree in the bedroll that evening, and rose before dawn and rode on.

The third day, they reached the Red River ferry and rode on into Denton. Belle had a cousin who farmed west of there. They avoided the town and rode out there. His name was Hugo Grimes. And from the scowl written on his sweaty face when he walked out of the corn patch where he'd been hoeing, he was not pleased at seeing her.

"What the gawdamn hell do you want?" he growled.

"I brought my man by to introduce him." She reined Jasper around to face him.

"Well, introduce him."

"This is Slocum. Meet my ill-mannered cousin Hugo Grimes."

Slocum nodded.

"I don't really care who you fuck. Have a good day." Grimes started back for his hoe.

Her quirt raised high, she spurred Jasper at him. Then she began flailing him over his head and shoulders with the quirt. "You ungrateful bastard. My folks fed you. They staked you to this farm. And you speak to me like that. If I was a man I'd shoot you!"

At last, Slocum, who had ridden after her, caught her whip hand and stopped her. Tears streamed down her face as she looked at Grimes and tried to jerk away from Slocum's iron grasp. "That ungrateful sumbitch needs to be beat to death."

"Belle, get hold of yourself."

"But—but—"

"Come on, we're leaving. Right now."

She drew in a deep breath, shook her head in dismay at Slocum, and then spurred Jasper out of the short corn plants and plowed ground. Slocum never looked back at the stunned wobbly-legged man holding his cheek where she'd drawn blood. He loped his horse after her.

Man, she had a temper.

# 9

Fort Worth, especially in the stockyard district, was crowded with cowboys wearing parts of old gray uniforms and with Mexican vaqueros. There was also no shortage of tinhorn gamblers and men under high-crown hats wearing suits. On their arrival, Belle bought a second-hand black dress that fit her bustline tight while the skirt portion flowed in generous folds.

She looked very fashionable in the new garment, something she knew how to do at little expense. Slocum didn't offer to tell her that the dress probably came from the undertaker's nearby—she could find that out for herself if she wanted to know. They took a room in Mrs. Coldwell's boardinghouse, and left the three horses at Randall's Livery.

Accompanied by Belle, Slocum gambled in various saloons, winning as well as losing. In these card games, he began to meet men in the trade and learn all he could about trail driving. At the end of the week, there was a shoot-out in the street, and both men suffered mortal wounds. According to a bystander one man was Clarence Smith or Schmid. The other, some said, was Cimarron Jake. Since Slocum knew neither of them, he and Belle strolled on to the White Elephant Saloon to find a fresh game of poker.

Three hours later, a new man joined the game. He was short, with an expensive felt hat and dressed in a tailored suit as he sat across the table from Slocum. His face was tanned from a million days spent in the sun, and the snowy mustache was curled at the ends. When his turn to deal came, he shuffled the cards and then tapped them on the table.

"My head man was shot today," he said. "He ain't going to live much longer. Good news is he got the man who shot his brother in the back. Cimarron Jack. A worthless no-account. But boys, I need a ramrod to take my herd north. I only came up this far to be sure they'd be all right. I got way too much to see after at home to take them to Kansas."

"I never caught your name," Slocum said as the man began dealing.

"Norm Ryder, Double RT Ranch, Dove City, Texas."

"Slocum's mine."

The man paused, looked hard at Slocum. His blue eyes began to twinkle. "Were you in this man's army?"

"Yes."

"Well, Slocum, meet me in the morning at Sally's diner. We can talk about it there. Say seven?"

"Fine," Slocum said, looking at his hand. When he glanced over at Belle, he noticed her form a smile in the corners of her mouth. They might have found their man.

In the boardinghouse later, she was undressed and bouncing on the bed with excitement. "You found him!"

"Hush. Someone might hear us."

She held out her arms for Slocum and when he came within reach, she pulled him onto the bed. If there ever was a woman without time for foreplay, Belle was the one. Scooting under him, she quickly inserted his half-hard erection inside her and spread her legs for his deep entry. Then her fingernails, like claws, dug into his back, and she hunched her ass up at him in such a wild fashion that she made the bed ropes scream.

"Hee haw! Kansas, here we come!"

"Maybe." Then he joined in her woolly behavior, and the bed rocked so hard underneath them that he began to wonder if it might collapse. And when he finally began to arch his back and come, his effort blew her mind away.

They met Ryder in Sally's the next morning. The large platters of fried eggs, ham, biscuits, and grits, plus cups of hot coffee, soon silenced their small talk.

"You ever been to Kansas?" Ryder asked.

"Some, but I figure there's trails out there by now been cut deep in that sod."

"Hell, yes, there must be. I knew last night I had a man that could muster the job."

"I'd give it my level best."

"And what'll you do when he pulls out?" Ryder asked Belle.

"I'll be the cook's helper. Don't worry about me."

"That's unusual. I don't think a woman should be out on a trail drive."

"Belle won't be a problem," said Slocum. "In fact, she should be an asset."

Ryder made a face, and then he shrugged.

"If she causes one problem, I'll send her back here quicker than you can shake a lamb's tail," said Slocum.

"I'll hold you to that," Ryder told him.

"What do you pay?"

"Fifty a month and five percent of the gross if you don't lose over ten percent of the cattle."

"We'll try to make that percentage." Slocum reached over and shook Ryder's hand.

"Them boys is holding the herd out west on the West Fork of the Trinity. I aimed to have the my supplies hauled out there and then send the herd north before my man got shot." Ryder dropped his chin and shook his head in defeat.

"We're sorry you've lost him, Mr. Ryder. Is there anything else we can do for you?" Slocum asked.

"I want to have some music for Clarence's funeral. Those

boys out there will want to be there. He was well liked by the crew. So I guess we'll bury him out there someplace."

"Mr. Ryder," Belle said, "if we can borrow or rent a piano and have it hauled out there, I can play anything you want to hear."

"You certain, Mrs. Slocum?"

She nodded. "Anything you want to hear."

Slocum agreed.

The next day, Slocum met the crew out on the windswept grassy hills west of Fort Worth.

Ryder told them about Clarence Schmid's fate, how he'd finally slipped away. Slocum saw some wet eyes and hard head shaking.

"Boys, we need to dig a grave. Slocum here, who'll be the new trail-drive boss, well, his wife Belle is coming with the piano I rented and she's going to play some hymns. Boys, I want this nice as we can get it. Clarence was a helluva fine hand and a good man. We'll miss him, but Slocum here will be the new boss. I expect you to work for him like you did Clarence."

Many swallowed hard, but they struck out their hands as Ryder introduced each one to Slocum.

"Pike Renegear, left point man." A lanky man in his thirties with golden straw hair and blue eyes shook Slocum's hand.

"Dawson McLain, right point rider. Been with me since before the war." A shorter man with a darker complexion, he wore an unblocked hat.

"Rube Goldman. Drover." Obviously, from his name he was Jewish. He had a warm smile to welcome Slocum and a firm handshake.

Bonner Day was pimple-faced and still in his teens, and he had a big grin for Slocum.

"Texas Jim Teal, he always has an extra gun if you run out," Ryder teased. The short man with a small mustache wore two six-guns.

"Blister Yates, horse wrangler." Another boy in his teens who looked like he wasn't dry behind the ears.

"Howdy, Slocum, I'm Coalie Frye, the cook," a short older man with a stiff leg and bushy white beard said, sticking out his hand.

"And here's Harvey Boyd. He's our fiddle." A big rawbone cowboy, Harvey stuck out a calloused large hand to shake with Slocum.

"That's the crew."

Slocum nodded. "I am glad to be here. I'll need all of your help to get up there. Now, we need a deep grave dug for Clarence. Get the shovels and picks and let's go to work. Belle will be here in an hour or so."

They all fell in, spelling each other, and a badger would have had a helluva time outdoing them. The grave was probably deep enough when someone said, "Listen, I hear music."

Ryder jumped to his feet and dusted off the seat of his pants. "I hear it, too."

"Rock of Ages" floated over the crotch-high grass, and Belle struck the ivory keys with the expertise of a concert pianist. Everyone began singing it, and by the time the black man driving the team reached the grave on the windswept hilltop, they were singing the next hymn, "Holy, Holy, Holy."

Hatless, with the strong south breeze ruffling their hair, the men went to the wagon and unloaded the coffin. They carried Clarence's remains over to the grave as Slocum went for ropes to lower it in. Belle never missed a beat, playing next "Faith of Our Fathers." The new pine box was lowered gently, and Ryder nudged Slocum to say something.

"Let us pray." Slocum dug deep. "Lord, we're sending you a friend of ours. To these young men, he was a father. To the rest, he was their leader in storms, stampedes, and all the bad rivers that they've crossed. Through all this strife and the trying times, Clarence Schmid, he was the boss and they all looked up to him. Now, he has crossed over and is in your country, Lord. Treat him well for he has earned his rest. And we know when we join him, Lord, that he'll have a great campsite picked out and firewood drug in. In his name we pray, Amen."

Ryder's hand clamped him on the shoulder. "They should have made you a damn general. That was good." Then he blew his nose as loud as a trumpet.

Quieter than before, Belle played "Amazing Grace." And Clarence Schmid was covered up.

Ryder waded over to her in his chaps and pulled off his hat, held it over his chest. "Ma'am, you can go on any trail drive I ever make. What do I owe you?"

She shook her head and turned to the driver. "Now. Mr. Cramer, you drive careful going back. We don't want anything to happen to this piano."

The black man nodded at her. "I's bet you could sure make some big money playing that piano for things like dis."

"I'd rather drive cattle." She let Slocum catch her by the waist and set her on the ground. "You be careful now with it."

"Yes, ma'am."

"I'll sure pay you, ma'am," said Ryder.

She hooked her arm in Slocum's. "I really want to go on this drive. That is enough. Don't worry about me."

When they were alone and away from the others, Slocum hugged her. "He'd've paid you."

She wrinkled her nose. "I'd've felt bad taking money for a church thing like that."

He hugged her shoulder. "You're a hard person to figure out at times."

"Well, don't try then. I gave up trying to figure you out way back there in Arkansas." She reached around and hugged his hips to hers. "We're both strange people, but we make good love."

Their supplies were loaded in the chuck wagon along with her sidesaddle and her dress, which was tucked in her bag. She wore men's canvas pants, suspenders, chaps, a man's collarless pullover shirt, a vest, and a plain cowboy hat still stiff out of the box.

"They say from the Red River crossing, it takes eight weeks to cross the Indian Territory and two weeks from the Kansas line to Abilene," Pike told Slocum while they ate supper, everyone seated cross-legged on the ground.

"That'll put us up there in August," Slocum said.

The other boys nodded.

"It'll take two months to come home with a chuck wagon, they say," Bonner told them, waving his fork.

"More coffee?" Belle asked, making the rounds with the pot.

"Yes, ma'am," Bonner said, holding out his tin cup. "Mighty kindly of you going along with us, ma'am, 'cept some of us will have to watch our tongues."

"There isn't much I have not heard," she said, teasing, and he blushed.

Slocum gave them the night watch list for that night, and the first shift went out to relieve the boys riding herd so they could eat. The rest rolled out their beds. They would move out come sunup.

He wondered if he could even sleep. It would be his job to find a campsite ten-twelve miles up the way toward the Red River crossing. Lots to do and think about. He'd have to learn a lot, too, before they got very far.

He took their bedroll off a ways from camp. "Well, to-morrow we roll," he said to Belle.

She sat on the bedroll and pulled off the boots he'd bought her. Rubbing her feet, she laughed. "A lot easier to take off than those shoes."

"Hell, I was just getting used to making love with you wearing them."

"Damn you, Slocum." She rose on her knees and began to pound on him.

He wrestled her down on the top of the roll, then kissed her and drove all the nonsense away. "You better get those britches off, girl."

She shook her head in disgust and wiggled out of them. Then she shed the vest and chose to wear the shirt. His hand slid under it and he felt her firm breasts. "Damn, girl, I'm sure glad you came along."

She nodded and worked herself underneath him, reached down, and inserted his cock inside her. "Here's why."

*Maybe so. Maybe so, Belle, darling.*

# 10

"Guess you'll catch up with me and find us a place to camp this evening?" Coalie asked, loading up his utensils and ready to pull out.

"Keep heading north. You can easily see the tracks." Slocum felt certain that the old tracks would be easy to follow. "Be sure there is some grazing there left for this herd."

"Sure thing. Blister can keep up with the remuda. He's a good boy."

"Have any trouble, let them come see me."

"Oh, we'll have 'em. See ya later, Boss." Then Coalie spit to the side and climbed up on the wagon. He unwound the reins off the brake and unlocked and was on his way. Slocum could hear the bell steer and all the bawling. Pike had the herd starting out.

Things looked all right. The cattle began to move out in a column. The lead steer was out in front. Belle joined Slocum on a ranch horse, riding like a man. She looked like a teenage boy under that new hat.

"It's all going smooth right now," she said, and grinned.

"That's right." He rubbed his left palm on his chaps to dry it. "I hope it holds."

Whips cracked like shots and the cattle, accustomed to the drive, continued to move. Cowboys crowded the lazy ones with their horses. Things were under way with lots of yelling and cursing at the stragglers.

"I'm going ahead and find us a campsite," Slocum said.

Belle agreed. "I'll fill in where I can help."

"Thanks." He rode on.

He short-loped wide of the herd, and watched his swing riders shaping the long serpentine line up. They knew their roles. Abilene, here we come.

The days dragged on with only a few incidents. A small stampede had the hands all up saddling horses in the starlight, but it was contained quickly. A thunderstorm rode the western sky one night and each man's horse was saddled and hobbled close by. Daytime temperatures grew hotter each day, the south wind did the same, and the dust, boiled up by eight thousand cloven hooves, rose like smoke from hell.

Slocum kept track of the days with a pencil and a logbook. He also noted down the losses he knew about.

What he worried the most about was Belle, but despite the trail dust and grit, she fit in well with the crew and Coalie. She fixed rice-and-raisin pudding while Coalie made supper many nights. Her cinnamon sugar rolls the boys considered a big treat, and she even found some wild plums to cook up for the hands.

She also sang along with the crew, and accompanied by Rube's harmonica and Harvey's fiddle. She even did a break down on the fiddle that drew their applause. She wrinkled her nose at the end for them doing that. "Why, that was not half as good as my uncle could play it."

Slocum figured they must be halfway across Indian Territory at the end of the month. He'd stay clear of the other herds, not wanting to sort out that many cattle. They'd even picked up strays all the way. Two or three here or there that heard or smelled his herd and came bawling across the hills to join them. Long as they didn't fight much to establish a place in the herd, he let them go along. But they were also the beef the crew ate since the cattlemen's brand inspector in Abilene would send the money for those critters to the brand owners and Ryder would get nothing for their care.

He'd heard once in Texas that the other fella's beef was always sweeter than your own. On this trip, he believed it.

One afternoon, he was helping Coalie set up camp when Texas Jim came busting his horse across the prairie. He reined up in a cloud of dust.

"We got us a passel of trouble, Boss. Injuns got us blocked. They want a hundred head to let us pass."

"A hundred head?" Slocum asked in disbelief.

Coalie echoed his question.

"Catch a fresh horse," Slocum said to the cowboy. "And we'll go up and see what's going on."

"Boss, them devils can be dangerous," said Coalie. "They'll sure fill your ass full of arrows if you ain't careful. Wonder if they're Comanch. They're the worst."

Slocum nodded. He was riding Big Man that day, one of his cut of the remuda. Big Man was a stout black horse he liked that could cover lots of ground in a day. Without grain for their horses, the crew used each horse only once every six days, and the ponies were fat on the grass. Texas Jim came back in, leading a fresh one he'd cut out from the herd and roped for himself. He quickly exchanged saddles, and they were off with Coalie still offering a lot of advice when they were beyond hearing him.

"How many bucks are there?" Slocum asked, upset by the notion that the Indians had blocked his herd.

"Several. They ain't armed impressively, but there might be twenty of 'em and they were yipping and making war cries. Pike told me to go find you and be quick about it."

"Good, I'll settle with them."

"Said that this was their land and we owed them rent."

"I wonder how much they like living above it." Slocum tried to rein in the growing anger building inside him.

"What do you mean?" Texas Jim shouted at him.

"I meant, how much do they enjoy living, huh?"

The cowboy grinned.

The cattle were spread out grazing when Slocum topped the rise. In the distance, he saw the paint ponies standing hipshot in a bunch, and noted the colorful feathers as well as the blankets the men wore.

Pike rode over to meet Slocum and Texas Jim. "Their main man is called Horse Who Runs. He says he gets rent from all the drovers that pass through here."

"Where's Belle?"

"She's with the boys riding around the cattle so they don't stampede if these bucks go crazy."

That was good. "Can we cut out ten strays with other brands to pay them with?"

Pike looked skeptically at him. "He said he wants a hundred head."

Slocum glanced off toward the Indians, wishing he'd brought a rifle from the wagon. He wouldn't be without one ever again. The bucks were dancing around and having a good time, like they'd already won. Some of those herd bosses passing through might have been pushovers. He damn sure wasn't.

He told the two drovers to stay where they were, and booted Big Man forward. Sitting down twenty or so feet in front of of the other Indians was a fat old buck who struggled to his feet and held a lance with feathers tied on the end.

"You bossy man?" he asked.

Slocum nodded.

"You must pay me hundred cows to use my land."

"I will pay you ten to cross it."

The old man with salt and pepper braids shook his head. "If you want to pass, you pay me hundred."

"Horse Who Runs, what if I just kill you and your bones rot out here? The wolves and the coyotes will chew on them."

"Hmm," he snuffed out of his nose. "I have more braves than you have."

"These men with me are Texans."

With a frown, the chief hit his own chest with his fist. "I am not afraid of Texans."

Slocum leaned over in the saddle. "They eat Injuns in Texas. There ain't no Injuns left where they live 'cause they ate them all."

Horse Who Runs talked in guttural words to two other bucks who came up to join him, and they argued. Finally, the chief shut them up and turned back. "We take ten head."

"Now, you can't kill them till we are over that rise with all of the rest of our herd." Slocum pointed to the rim north of them.

Horse Who Runs folded his arms over his potbelly. "Why you say that?"

"'Cause you'll kill them like they were buffalo and that will stampede my herd."

He nodded. "No kill till you are gone."

Slocum cupped his hands over this mouth to shout. "Pike! Get the boys to work in easy and cut out ten head of strays! Rope and drag them out if you have to, but don't booger the herd!"

"We can do that! You safe out there?"

"Safe enough for now!"

Pike and Texas Jim rode off. Slocum dismounted and found a fistful of cigars in his saddlebags. He walked over to hand them out to the three bucks.

"You got any gawdamn whiskey?" Horse Who Runs asked.

"No whiskey." Slocum shook his head. There was some in the chuck wagon, but he carried none. Besides that, he was paying this old sumbitch about eight hundred dollars worth of beef for his rent. If they came off his own cattle count, he'd really be pissed.

The sorting took some time. Slocum and the three bucks sat on the ground and smoked up his cigars. There wasn't much to talk about. Horse Who Runs said the agency had lied to him and had had no food for them since winter. There were few buffalo this year, and they would starve if they didn't charge the cattle drivers rent.

At last, Slocum could see Belle with the several others crowding a small bunch of steers toward them. Under her hat and garb, she looked like one of the crew. Horse Who Runs nodded, rose stiffly, and walked back, waving his hands and giving orders. No doubt saying that they couldn't slaughter the steers until the herd was gone. Slocum hoped so.

The bucks took charge of the stock. Slocum told Pike to start heading their herd out. The Indians drove their wards westward, and Belle rode in close to him.

"You talk their language?"

He shook his head.

"How did you get them down from a hundred?"

He winked at her. "I told him these Texas cowboys were cannibals and ate all the Indians in Texas. He must have believed me 'cause he cut his demands. They aren't supposed to kill them till we get gone."

She frowned at him.

"Hell, they'll do it like a buffalo hunt and spook our herd, too."

"Well, good night—good that you knew that—Boss Man."

"We better help move this herd on."

She smiled and rode off to join the others.

Slocum rode in and assisted them. Soon, they were striking out with his swing riders in place. The snakelike formation took shape and the drovers took their places.

When they crossed the last rise and Slocum reined up, the cow hunt began. Above the wind, he could hear the war cries and see the lancers spearing the cattle while on horseback like they did with the buffalo. Their hunt was short-lived and he turned Big Man north again.

His *cannibals* would have something to talk about in camp that night. He laughed until he about cried while loping over the rolling grassland. The streams they had to cross from there on, Pike had promised him, would be rock-bottomed. He liked that. In three weeks, they should be in Kansas. The summer was going fast.

With the longhorns at last grazing or chewing their cuds, the weary hands came into camp. Most napped before they drew their nightly guard duty riding around the herd. Belle met Slocum at the wagon. When she drew him away from the rig, she asked, "Could we go up or down this creek that we're camped on and find me a place to bathe? I stink like a horse and am twice as dirty as a dust devil."

He agreed and, after telling Coalie they'd be back, they rode off by themselves. It wasn't their first separation from the wagon for this purpose, but it had been several days since they'd done it. Slocum felt guilty that in his hard push northward he'd neglected doing this so long.

The pool of water he found upstream was isolated. Satisfied they were alone, and with the horses hitched, they undressed and slipped into the waist-deep water, where Belle swam. Her snowy white body looked like a river otter in the stream. Then, she returned and he gave her the bar of soap.

When she finished bathing, she washed her hair with a special shampoo that she kept in a cork-lid bottle and that she said was made from yucca roots. Then, after using the small towel he carried and drying in the hot afternoon sunshine, they lounged on a canvas groundsheet that he carried behind his saddle for such purposes.

"Well, are you tired of driving cattle yet?" he asked, playing with her right boob.

"Tired? Lands, no. What kind of Indians were those today?"

"I never bothered to ask them." He glided his hand over her smooth belly and nested it down in her stiff pubic hair.

She twisted toward him. "I figure there are little kids who went to sleep tonight with their bellies full."

As they lay side by side, he moved against her, then reached over and squeezed her tight ass. "I bet there were."

"How did you figure out to give them the strays?"

"Just luck, I guess."

"No! Slocum, it wasn't luck. You are a sly old boy and I'm learning from you. Now, if you do not get on top of me, I'm going to scream."

"Oh." He grinned down at her and did like she ordered. Like he had been told.

# 11

Some hard-looking cowboys came by their camp the next evening. None of the three were kids. They were unshaven, their clothes worn out. Slocum told them to drop down and have supper. Coalie always had enough food, though he usually made a fuss about feeding strays. These weren't the first, but Slocum considered them the most likely to be up to no good.

The leader, a thin man in his late thirties, called himself Cy, and he introduced the other older one as Twig and the younger one as Burl. Slocum introduced a few of his men who were eating, and then he sat down again with Belle.

The cowboys filled the plates Coalie handed out, and Belle made a face at Slocum. "Why not introduce me?"

"I don't like them." Then she and Slocum spoke in low tones.

"You think they may be trouble?"

"I'm not certain, but I'm not turning my back on 'em."

"Good idea."

"You know them?"

"I think the leader rode with Quantrill during the war. Cy wasn't his name then."

Slocum nodded.

82

"You all been up to the railhead?" Slocum asked them aloud.

Cy nodded with his mouth full of food. "Yeah, we been there."

"Just wondering. You sell some cattle?"

Cy shook his head. "We was passing through is all."

"Headed for Texas?"

"Mister, I guess we'll go anywhere we gawdamn well please."

"Hey, I was just being curious. Figured you knew more about this world than we did. Us eating dust and shagging after cattle all day."

Cy put down his plate, rose, and nodded, then started for the chuck wagon. Halfway there, he spun around and drew his gun. "First sumbitch moves is dead."

The other two had set their plates aside and drawn their guns.

"Now we want all the money and watches that you have," Cy said.

"Listen, you kinda caught us short," Slocum said. "We ain't coming from Abilene. We're going up there."

"Listen, Boss Man, or whatever they call you. I want all your money and be quick. You, kid—holy shit, you ain't a boy." Cy walked over and jerked off Belle's hat. "Look here, boys, we've done got us a little darling."

Twig grinned and rubbed his hand over his crotch. Then he held out the cotton sack for Texas Jim to put his money in. The coins jingled going in. The look on Texas Jim's face would have melted iron.

"Who are you fellas?" Rube asked, putting some folding money in the bag.

"Robbers," Twig said, and laughed at their plight.

"You better make a wide loop of me," Dawson McLain said. "We ever cross tracks again, you'll be pushing up daisies." He added more to their sack.

"You sorry ungrateful bastards," Coalie said with his hands on his hips.

"Shut up, old man. Get over here, darling," Cy said, indicating to Belle that he wanted her where he stood beside the wagon.

Bonner Day used his finger to point. "You lay a hand on that lady and you're a dead man."

"Why, boy, you ain't even got a gun talking big like that. Shut your mouth and sit down before I waste some .45 ammo on you."

"I'm telling you, mister—"

Under the threat of Cy's gun, Bonner sat down, fuming.

Belle walked over and stood by him. "What's your name, honey?" he asked looking her over.

"Myrabelle Shirley Younger."

"Younger?" Cy cut a hard look at Slocum. "You ain't a Younger. Myra Belle Shirley, huh? I knew some Shirleys at Carthage before the war."

"Those were my parents."

"So who're you married to, Jim or Cole?"

"Cole."

"Where's he at and why're you with this cow outfit?"

Hands on her hips, she glared at the outlaw. "Mess with me and you'll find out."

"You've got lots of spunk. I might want a turn or two with you for old time sake. So you're Cole Younger's wife?"

"Mister, I'm warning you. You better leave here and keep riding."

"You're warning me? Why, you sassy little bitch—" He backhanded her and the slap knocked her into the wagon. Holding her face, she crumpled to her knees.

Coalie jumped on the wagon wheel, reached in, drew out the shotgun, cocked the hammers, and blew Cy away. As if on cue, the others grappled with the remaining pair and sent them to the ground, pounding them with their angry fists.

Slocum, seeing the others were taking care of the outlaws, went over and lifted Belle to her feet. "You all right?"

"I'll be fine. Let me go hug Coalie. He saved my life."

"Maybe all of our lives." Slocum turned her loose and

walked over to the hands who were holding the bandits on the ground.

"What we going to do with 'em?" Bonner asked.

"There's a big walnut down by the creek. We're going to hang 'em."

Everyone nodded.

Small bits of conversation were exchanged as the fierce tension began to drain from everyone. Slocum walked back to where the red-faced cook stood with Belle hugging him.

"Why, missy, when he slapped you, I didn't care if I died. I was first kind of afraid of hitting you, but with you on the ground, I had a clear shot."

"You are a wonderful hero," she said, and kissed Coalie's forehead again.

Slocum shook his hand. "Thanks."

"Sure thing. Boys, just tie them two up. I've got rice and bugs to celebrate."

So they sat on the ground and ate their sweetened rice-and-raisin pudding.

Then they took Cy's body to hang alongside the rest of his gang. Burl, the youngest, begged them to turn him loose, saying he'd never do another criminal thing in his life.

"Sure," Bonner said. "That's until you get over the next rise."

"No, I swear. I swear on my mother's grave. I'm only sixteen. Give me another chance. Oh, dear God. Where's Younger's wife? Ma'am, save me, please."

"You can rot in hell!" Belle said, and a cheer went up.

Nooses were tossed over the tree limb, their hands were tied behind their backs, and wearing their neckties, the outlaws were piled on their horses. Slocum asked for their last words. Twig went first.

"I don't deserve to die here. Ain't you boys got no respect for a man who give his life for the Confederacy?"

"No," Bonner said, holding his horse by the bridle.

"Oh, dear God, make them see. I am an innocent boy. Please spare me 'cause I want to live, Lord," Twig cried.

Slocum held a coiled lariat in his hand behind Burl's horse. Pike stood ready behind Twig's. When they shouted and slapped the two horses on the ass, the two outlaws dangled in silence with broken necks, and then their dead leader, Cy, was drawn up beside them.

In silence, Slocum and his crew walked back to camp.

"What will we do with their horses and saddles?" one of the crew asked.

"When we get to Abilene, those without mounts of their own and worse rigs can put their names in a hat and we'll draw for them."

"Thanks," Rube said.

Belle agreed. In the bloody sundown's glare, she hung onto Slocum's arm while going to camp. "Guess I blabbed my mouth off today."

"No problem. Those cowboys don't give a damn who you're married to. You're one of them now and from Coalie on down, they'd 've all done what they could for your protection. I was worried Bonner might try. something foolish, he was so upset."

She nodded.

So they drove on north the next day. Mile by mile, they made ten to twelve of them a day, then halted to graze the cattle to keep flesh on them. All day in the saddle and then with a couple hours herd duty at night, his trail hands were as worn out and cranky as some of the horses in the remuda. The cow ponies had the most rest of any, so they could really get ready to buck.

After they crossed the Canadian, Slocum declared a day off to repair saddles and bridles, take a bath in the river, wash their clothes, and shave. Coalie gave some haircuts. Belle took her leave of the men at mid-morning, and returned in a few hours looking sparkling.

Everyone relaxed. They lounged around camp. Belle made double batches of her cinnamon rolls and the day passed too fast. That evening, on top of her in the bedroll, Slocum gently enjoyed the pleasures of her body, plunging in and out of her cunt, raising her fever enough that the contracting walls began to test him. She threw her legs up in the air and let him go to the bottom of her well until at last he came. Then, they collapsed in a pile.

"Now, if we had time to do that in the morning, I'd really like cattle driving," she said.

Kneeling over her, he tweaked her nose and chuckled. "You never get enough."

"Oh, I do for a while."

"A short while."

At dawn, they were headed north. Men spoke of the Arkansas crossing. So far, the Red River had been the worst, but that day was long forgotten—no men, horses, or cattle had been lost. The Arkansas could be low or raging since it came from the Colorado Rockies and any big rain out there would come roaring down the Arkansas. When Slocum rode up to scout it, he felt good. It was low. Probably at the mid-summer level, even lower than he had expected. He crossed it and then went up to the store, saloon, and whorehouse on the north bank—a place they called Wichita Crossing.

He hitched his horse at the rack and went inside. A young girl on the second-story balcony leaned over the railing and said, "Hi."

He waved and went to the bar.

"You need company?" she asked from the head of the stairs.

"No."

"Well, you need some, you just whistle, I'll come running."

"Thanks," he said, and ordered a double shot of good whiskey.

"Heading for Abilene, I guess?" The bartender filled the double shot glass and waited with the bottle in his hand.

"Yes, the herd's behind me. We should cross here day after tomorrow."

"Been lots of cattle go by here this summer. Never thought

Joe McCoy's deal would work like it has, but it's been slick as a gut."

"Two weeks up the road?" Slocum asked.

"About that. There's cattle herds scattered all over waiting for railcars. There's a backup. You might want to ride in and look it over."

Slocum raised the glass to the man. "Thanks for the information."

He downed the rest, and it cut a path through his throat. "They play poker in here?"

"There's a game about every night."

"Good. I might drop by."

"I'll look for you. Name's Floyd Cantrell."

"Might fine meeting you. Mine's Slocum." They shook hands. He paid the man and went back out in the hot afternoon. One thing he'd found being nearly the last herd coming north for the year was that there was plenty of heat. The wind on his face felt like it came from the fires of hell when he mounted up.

He trotted down to the shallow-running Arkansas, crossed the ford, and headed back for the camp. One thing he had noticed in the saloon was the piano. Belle might enjoy playing it while he sat in on a few hands of cards.

Coalie was busy preparing supper. How that short man with his bad leg could set up the wagon, toss off the bedrolls, put up the canvas fly, and build a fire in such short time was beyond Slocum. Coalie said it was easier than putting up with some dumb kid he had to tell how to do everything time and again. Besides—he liked doing it.

Slocum helped himself to some coffee, and squatted down close to the side board. "Who invented this system for fixing a chuck wagon?"

"They say ole Charlie Goodnight, the ex-ranger, did. They started making these setups to fit in these army wagons in San Antonio this past winter. I told the main man, Mr, Ryder, I wanted one, and we went down there and I designed them shelves so my stuff would fit."

Coalie spit off to the side. "Sure makes it lots easier. I went to Sedalia, Missouri, last year with a greasy sack outfit. I'd never do that again."

"What do you mean? Never go to Missouri?"

"I never left nothing up there to go back after. Those bastards are crazy. We finally got through with four hundred head. Half of what we started with. And I ain't ever again taking no greasy-sack outfit anywhere either."

"Greasy-sack?" Slocum shook his head at the man, a little amused at his storytelling.

"Yeah, you pack it all—" He spit tobacco juice aside again. "You carried it all in gunnysacks on packhorses. I hated it. That's why I smile so much about this wagon."

Slocum blew on his coffee. That would be a mess to cook from. "I see your point. What do you do for Ryder in the winter?"

"I make plow points and put handles in double shovels. Worked on this wagon getting it in shape. He found work for me and I liked the outfit. If we hadn't got through with them last year and he hadn't sold them high, guess he'd've lost his place. It was hell. Ask Pike."

"Why ain't Pike the trail boss?"

Coalie shook his head. "He's a tough man, but he ain't a leader. He'd fight wildcats beside ya, but he ain't a boss and knows it. On last year's drive to Sedalia, we fought bald knobbers and rustlers all the way up there, and that's in timber, too. No wagon, only packhorses. Bad deal. 'Course they stampeded our herd through rail fences and then here would come a damn farmer wagging a scattergun. It was a wonder we ever made it up there."

"That flint rock was hard on 'em, too?"

"By damn, one thing, it got their feet so sore they finally won't run. We even had to abandon several steers on account of that. But we delivered what we had left and went home to Texas with plenty of money to meet his obligations. And we got our pay, too."

"Times like those are good."

"Amen."

"What did Ryder need to get back there for this time?"

Coalie put his hands on his hips and spit off in the knee-high grass. "Got him a new bride last winter. His first wife died during the war. Had him a Mexican woman—well, he lived with Carla and they had two kids along with his four by the first wife. Met this white woman in San Antonio—oh, she's fancy and he married her. She moved in, Carla moved out, and so did his two kids with her. I took them to San Antonio and set them up. Poor woman was beside herself. 'How could he do this to me?'"

Slocum nodded. He could hear the cattle lowing in the south. He checked the sun time. Mid-afternoon. "You tell her?"

"I could have told her how, but he's got him a real headache with this Angela. Guess you'll meet her this fall. It's damn peaceful out here compared to that ranch any more." Coalie spit again.

Belle rode in and swung down. She took off her hat and fanned her face. "Hot one today. Cattle are out eating or resting. Boys are coming in."

"Any trouble?"

She shook her head and squatted beside him in the fly's shade. "How far away is the river? I need a bath."

"A good hour or more north."

"Is there a creek I can cool off in? The one the cattle watered at back there isn't much to bathe in." Still using her hat for a fan, she looked red-faced.

"Let's go see. We'll be back," he said to Coalie.

"I sure hope you're coming back." Then he laughed.

They rode off to find her a water hole.

"Are you getting antsy about getting this drive over with?" she asked as they rode side by side in a long trot.

"Antsy? What do you mean?" He frowned at her.

"You seemed restless to me these past few days. Like you have something on your mind."

"You seeing behind my eyes again?"

She shook her head. "No, I've known since you let me come along that someday you'd be gone."

"I hope not until after Abilene and the cattle are sold."

"What will you do then?"

"I'm not sure. You know I've told you word spreads and someone sees a wanted poster."

"Federal?"

He nodded.

"That could be serious. I really am sorry now that I had you play Cole Younger."

"No problem. What happened to him?"

"Gawdamnit, he just up and left me. No word. No note. I guess I tried to cover up my shame by saying you were him for my kinfolks. No, damn it, I was mad and I didn't want anyone saying, 'Poor Belle, she can't keep a man.'"

"You call that pride," he said.

"He busted my pride."

"He was a damn fool and your image will haunt him the rest of his life."

She stared over at him as he reined up.

"What's wrong?" she said.

"The creek is a short way up here. Let's walk. I like the contact with you."

Her shiny wet face beamed at his words.

With his arm over her shoulder, they led their snorting horses and ambled along in the thin dust from thousands of hoofprints that had cut the sod. "This was a nice idea. I guess I needed this. How did you know I did?"

He bent over and kissed her. She tasted like the eternal acrid dust with a sweetener of her own added.

"You know I haven't gotten mad in days?" she asked.

"I noticed that."

She wrinkled her nose. "I been too damn tired to get mad. You know Bonner is getting married when he gets back to Texas?"

"Lucky gal, huh?"

"He'll make a good one. He wants a ranch. Says he's going to carve one out. I bet he does. Why can't I find me some fella that isn't wanted or the law ain't chasing?"

Slocum laughed. "They ain't exciting enough for impatient you."

Acting mad at his words, she elbowed him in the side as they walked up on the stream. "I suppose you're right. They are not exciting enough for me. This water hole looks good enough. Let's jump in."

He found the towel and soap in his saddlebags, then untied the ground cloth from behind the cantle. He'd need it, too. After Abilene, what would he do?

# 12

Slocum's crew crossed the Arkansas and laughed. After so many yarns told around camp about the half-mile-wide raging river and quicksand at the crossing, they kept asking Slocum if it was really the mighty Arkansas River. He nodded with, "That's all there is this time."

But he'd seen the debris from past floods in treetops, and knew she could sure run out of her banks. A hundred plus miles to go and he had lost only a few cattle and nary a hand. God help him.

"I can stake a man to two dollars from his wages if he wants to go over to that saloon and store we passed back there. But we have to night herd and not be so drunk you fall off your horse and spook the whole herd."

They laughed. An uneasy laugh, like the men didn't know if they should laugh at his words or not. But they must have found his words funny.

"Go in there three at a time. Stay together. These places are like rat dens. No law in this country. The scum that rides the waves of the western advance are killers, and would do so for a quarter 'cause they have no conscience. We met their kind back there in our own camp."

Bonner, Pike, and Dawson won with the longest straws. Slocum gave them the money. Bonner rode by and spoke to Belle. "Miss Belle, you need anything from town?"

"No, Bonner, but you better mail her that letter I wrote for you."

Leaning out of the saddle, he clapped his vest pocket and then straightened. "I sure will first thing, and thanks a lot. Susie Ann'll die getting it. She knows I can't write nothing."

Belle came back to the wagon shaking her head. "Ain't that boy a hoot?"

Coalie spit off in the grass and came back, wiping his mouth on his sleeve. "How come a boy as bright as Bonner can't read and write?"

"Said his folks during the war never stayed in one place long enough to enroll him in school. Then he got too big to go to class."

"It's a damn shame. Damn shame."

Belle agreed. "When are we going to town?"

Seated cross-legged on the ground, Slocum rubbed his palms on his chaps. "Tonight. I want to play some poker."

"What can I do?"

"They've got a piano. No more business than he has, I figure you can play it to your heart's content."

She wet her sun-dried lips. "That sounds amazing. You noticed it?"

"Talked to the man in there about the cattle business and saw it sitting in the corner."

She jumped over, knocked his hat off, and kissed him. "That is really nice of you."

"We'll see."

"Oh, what if it doesn't work?"

He held up his hands in surrender. "I don't know anything about a piano. Never tried it."

With a smirk written on her face, she bobbed her head confidently. "It has to work."

God. He hoped it did.

*   *   *

They were all eating supper in the late afternoon when Blister jumped up looking west. "They're coming back—already."

"About time," Slocum said between bites off a hot biscuit, and smiled at the others.

"Something's wrong, Slocum," Blister said. "Bonner is coming in belly down over his horse."

Slocum frowned at Belle and she shook her head. He set down his tin plate and went to see what was wrong. The others followed.

"What's wrong with Bonner?" Slocum asked Pike, who was leading his horse.

"He's dead."

"Dead?" Slocum could not believe it.

Pike nodded woodenly. "Dawson and I were in the saloon having a drink. Bonner went over to mail that letter Belle wrote for him at the store and to eat some peaches. Said he wasn't drinking. You know, he was all heated up about that girl back home.

"We heard shots. Ran out to see why, and two fellas were gunning him down and they rode out before Dawson and me could do a damn thing. The storekeeper told us Bonner was out on the stoop eating his first can of peaches when these two rode up and asked him something. Then the store man heard one of them cuss and say, 'You're a damn Reb.' Then they began shooting him."

Dawson made a sour face. "We never had chance to really see 'em or do a thing about it. They rode off before we even figured it out. Sorry, Boss, but we were just in frozen shock that anyone would do such a thing."

Belle was talking to Blister when Slocum looked around for her. She stepped over to Slocum, cold-faced. "I sent him for two fresh horses for us to ride."

He nodded. "Coalie, find us some jerky and some biscuits. Belle and I are going after his killers."

She nodded and ran to the wagon. When she emerged, she held two Spencer repeating rifles.

Slocum nodded at her actions and turned to his two oldest hands, Pike and Dawson McLain. "Move the herd east or west of this crossing so you don't get them mixed with another herd coming by. That would be a mess to sort."

Both men nodded.

"We aren't back in a week, then it will be up to you two to drive them to Abilene and get the best price you can for them for Ryder."

Pike drew in a deep breath and then, looking strained, he said, "Between Dawson and Coalie and me, we'll do it. Coalie can count better'n any of us."

"All right, I'm making you, Pike, the trail boss. You all have your jobs. It'll be tough without Bonner and with me being gone, but Coalie can pick campsites good as I can. Whatever you do, don't let anyone mix their herd with ours."

The grim-faced crew agreed.

"Now, bury Bonner. Belle and I are going after his killers before the trail gets too cold."

He wanted to go hug the downcast Pike and Dawson— tell 'em it was all right, nothing they could have done. But it still wouldn't have lifted the burden they felt. They bore the pain of not stopping Bonner's killers.

It was after dark when Slocum dismounted at the store. There was a light on inside.

"That the saloon's got the piano?" Belle asked.

"Yes. I'm going in here."

"Fine. I'm going to see how it plays."

His shoulders gave a shudder of revulsion, but he quickly nodded, realizing she needed some relief, too. Bonner was dead. The man she wrote the letter for to his sweetheart. Slocum went inside the store.

"Just closing up. Can I help you, sir?" the balding man asked, taking off his apron.

"A boy was shot today on your porch?"

"Yes. What a terrible tragic thing. Was he kin to you?"

"He was one of my crew. We have a herd. I was his boss.

He came to mail a letter to his sweetheart and eat some peaches."

The man swallowed hard. "He mailed that letter."

"I figured he did. These two men shot him, did you know them?"

"I don't think so. When I looked out, there was lots of gun smoke and that made it hazy. Then I ducked for my life. Sorry. I am not steady under gunfire."

"Neither am I. What kind of horses were they riding?"

"Bays, I think. It was all so fast and really I was afraid for myself. I am so sorry."

"Think. Think hard. One thing that you saw that will help me find them."

The man looked hard at the floor, which was made of rough-cut lumber. The grooves from the sawmill blades were beginning to be worn off under the gritty traffic. Then he looked up. "One of them had a soldier's cap. Yes, I can see him now. Not a cowboy hat, but a Union cap."

"Young? Old?"

"I'm sorry, that's all I can recall seeing." The man turned and a shocked look paled his face. "That's church music I'm hearing. 'Amazing Grace' on that piano over there."

"Yes, the lady playing it was a good friend of Bonner."

"But he said—"

"He wasn't going to marry this woman. She wrote the letter for him."

"I see. Felix Holms, sir, is my name. Is there anything else I can do for you?"

Slocum shook his head and left, unhitched his horse, and started for the saloon. The piano's tinny notes wafted out into the night. *Amazing grace, how great thou art . . .*

# 13

A male coyote fifty yards away from them dodged through the stems, his smoky coat coming into view. A red tongue lolled out. Then he was lost again in the tall grass. He was on his way home from a night of hunting. The purple cast of sunup spread across the rolling land.

"Those are buffalo out there." Slocum pointed them out to Belle. The brown globs that dotted the wide swale were bison.

"Lots of them," she said.

He agreed, grateful they weren't headed for his herd. He hoped to find an individual who had seen someone wearing a blue forager cap. They weren't as common anymore as they had been right after the war. Maybe they were common in Kansas. Common or not, he wanted the boy's killers.

"Is that smoke?" she asked, pointing to the slight streak in the sky.

"I've been watching it. It's someone's fire. Over on that far hillside. Let's lope. I'd like to know if the killers came by here."

When they drew closer, he could see the log ridgepole of a dugout. Piles of stiff buffalo hides were stacked on a two-wheel cart, and more were stretched on the ground all over the place. A few slinky, black Indian dogs bared their teeth and barked at Slocum and Belle.

Slocum held his hand out for Belle to get behind him. A squaw in her teens raised the buffalo hide door, and her dark eyes peered at them. Then she dropped it back in place.

"Well, who in the hell are they?" a loud bass voice demanded.

Then the speaker appeared with a Sharps rifle in his right hand. He was over six feet tall, and his shoulder-length reddish brown hair and full beard hid all but his cold blue eyes. He stepped outside, dressed only in a pair of leather pants. Barefooted and with his hairy chest, he seemed more animal than man.

"Who in the hell are you?"

"Name's Slocum. I'm looking for two men passed here earlier."

"What the hell for?"

"They shot one of my drovers."

"Maybe he needed it."

"He was unarmed, seated on the store's porch eating a can of peaches and minding his own business." Slocum heard the edge in his own voice.

"Well, sweet Jesus, the only ones went by here today are Sam and Gopher Dayton."

"One of them wear a Union cap?"

"Sam does."

"Where do they live?"

"They've got a wagon and outfit camped down on Soda Crick. What are you and that boy going to do?"

"The Bible says an eye for an eye."

"I done read it. But you and that boy ain't got enough metal to take them two on plus their Messikin skinners." He used the Sharps to casually point to Belle.

Slocum ignored his referral to her as a boy. "Our war ain't with the skinners."

"Want it or not—they're liable to join in."

"I guess you wouldn't know a man needed work?" Slocum asked.

He scratched his unkempt scalp and looked at the ground. "Kinda work that you're talking about will cost ya."

"How much?"

"Twenty bucks in silver or gold. I don't take paper money."

Slocum nodded. Having this sharpshooter along might be worth that. "I can afford you. Why're you willing to do this?"

He set the rifle down and took the beaded, fringed, leather shirt from the young squaw who'd slipped out to give it to him. "It's a cash market for hides. Their hides ain't no different to me than a buff."

"My name's Slocum. That's Belle." He indicated her with a head toss.

"My name's Elijah Stokes. They call me Hider, Hider Stokes." With the shirt on, he turned sideways, unlaced his pants, drew out a dick bigger then an elephant's, and pissed a big stream. Shaking it off and putting it away, he nodded. "Glad to meet you two. Willow's gone to get my horse. She's Arapaho." He shook his head whimsically. "I sure had some bad luck with squaws this past year—one died birthing, another got gored by a wounded buffalo, the third was killed by renegades who came by and stole my hides as well."

Hider sat on the ground and pulled on his moccasins.

"You get her killers?" Slocum asked.

"Sure did. I staked 'em out for the wolves to eat."

"Did the wolves find 'em?"

"Yeah. I sat on a rise a-watching, making sure no one came by and released them. It was a moonlit night. Took them wolves a while to make up their mind about eating them though. The four of them cussing and screaming to scare them off." When his footgear was on, Hider stood up.

"You know what a hungry wolf goes for first on a naked man staked out on the ground?"

Slocum shook his head.

"They go for his privates like they do underside of an animal in the flank. They tore off their dick and balls first. One man at a time." Hider grinned. "You could have heard them in St. Louis they screamed so loud. You don't die nice like that. Takes forever. Them sumbitches sure won't steal no one else's hides ever again."

Slocum nodded and turned to Belle with a head shake. She looked at the clear sky for help.

The squaw came running back with Hider's paint horse. His ears were cropped half off. He was an Indian pony and one used for buffalo hunting. With a pouch slung over Hider's shoulder and a shapeless wide-brimmed hat on his head, he hopped on his horse bareback and waved his rifle for Slocum and Belle to follow him.

"Damn," Belle said under her breath, and swallowed hard. "Old Donkey Dick is sure one tough hombre."

Slocum agreed, and they fell in behind their new guide. Hider finally reined up on a ridge and pointed to some downed buffalo and the men working them.

"That's their crew."

"Where are the two men?"

"Getting drunk, I'd say. They shoot the day's kill for their skinners, then go back to camp and get drunk."

"So we're letting them get real drunk?" Slocum asked. He wasn't opposed to that idea.

Hider grinned and winked at them. "Making it easy anyhow. Let's go see what them Messikins know."

Slocum agreed. They rode up on the two men and a boy trying to jerk a hide off a partially skinned bull with a team of small mules.

One man was lashing the mules with the lines, and the pair would hit their collars and then stagger to their knees.

"Hold up, amigos. You need to cut more hide loose before them small mules can do the job." Hider jumped in and began using his thin-bladed knife to separate the buffalo's hide from the meat and fat.

"There, boy. Now pull it harder," he said to the youth, who grinned at him. "Sumbitches, they don't savvy any English. They're worse than a Sioux squaw I had. She never listened either."

Hider waved at the teamster to start pulling again. This time with Hider and the boy slicing to separate hide from meat here and there, they began to peel it off the carcass. A shout went up when the team took charge, and the other man ran over to shake Hider's hand he was so grateful.

"Where's the Dayton brothers?" Hider asked the oldest man.

The man turned up his palms and shook his head. "No savvy."

"*Patrón?*" Slocum said from horseback.

"Ah." Then a burst of Spanish and the brown skinned man pointed south.

"He must mean in camp," Slocum said.

"Well, we can find that," Hider said with a confident smile.

They left the three, and Hider led the way south. When they topped the next rise, two wagons with weathered brown canvas tops sat parked by a creek. The wind twisted the smoke from their campfire. A woman in a red skirt and white blouse raised up from her cooking, and her eyes flew open in shock at the sight of the riders.

She shouted to someone out of sight and Hider swore. "Now they know we're coming. Damn her!"

Slocum waved Belle to move aside so she was wide of him, and checked the action of his Spencer. He rode more right of Hider, whose pony had begun to act anxious, like he knew something was up. He danced on his front feet. Hider growled at him—to no avail.

"He thinks we're going hunting."

"I see that," Slocum said.

"They break out their Sharps, we could be right in their sights. But I'm thinking they'll bring out their pistols to greet us. If they're drunk enough, that would be all right."

"Why?" Slocum asked.

"First, they ain't afraid of us and it's natural to use a handgun against another man. They only use them big guns for killing a buff."

"That you, Hider?" the tall one in the army cap shouted at them above the wind, pulling up his suspender on the left side and packing a big Walker Colt in his other hand as he came around the wagon.

"I ain't got no brother, Dayton." Hider's horse was side-stepping by this time.

"Who's with you?"

"A man named Slocum and a woman named Younger."

"What do they want?"

"They're buying hides." They finally drew their horses up fifty feet from the pair.

"Hell, why didn't you say so? We'd sell them some hides if they're paying a good price for 'em."

"I told 'em you would. I thought ten bucks a hide out here was a fair price."

Coughing his head off, the second brother came in view. Bent over, he stopped, half choked on his own phlegm. Red faced, out of breath, at last he blinked at Slocum and Belle.

"They ain't"—his cough got him again—"hide buyers."

"Who're they?" Sam asked, his look at his brother becoming to serious.

"Texas trail drovers. Damn Rebs like that kid we shot yesterday at the crossing."

Hider spurred his horse in close, skidded it to a stop, and fired his .50-caliber into Sam's chest. The impact of the huge bullet blew the man backward. Then Hider swung his horse around with his knees, drew a large knife from inside his shirt, and threw it.

Slocum was never sure where it came from. The knife went up to the hilt into Gopher's chest.

Gopher staggered around in a circle, gurgling, holding the knife's handle, unable to extract it. Finally, Hider booted his horse in and gave him a shove forward with his moccasin. The man fell facedown and babbled his last.

Matter-of-factly, the big man swung down, jerked Gopher's limp arm and threw him over onto his back, and retrieved his knife with a foot on the man's chest. He wiped the blood off on the man's clothing.

"I guess them Messikins will work for me now that I've got two wagons, four big mules, and lots of hides to sell. Hey, you women get out here."

Two fear-filled faces showed around the corner of the wagon. Hands to their mouths, they stepped out into view.

"Either of you speak English?" Hider asked.

Slocum and Belle dismounted. They listened close, and finally one of the women said, "I savvy some *inglés.*"

"What are your names?" Hider asked.

"I am Gloria and she is Marrettia."

"Who are you?" Hider asked.

"We are the wives of the men who work for them, Julio and Pablo. They are skinners, no?"

"I see that," Hider said. "What did you do for them?"

"The big one—Sam—he promise us work and big pay and good food. But we see no pay. We eat buffalo all the time. And they make us be their *putas* everyday."

Hider looked at Slocum for a translation of her words.

"Be their whores," Slocum said.

"I won't do that to you. You can work for me. You understand?"

"*Sí, señor.*" And they both curtsied for him.

Belle was standing over Sam Dayton, who was lying on his back with the black hole in his chest. He looked into forever out of blank eyes at the cloudless sky. She raised the quirt strapped on her left wrist and began flailing his corpse with it. The smacks of her strikes carried above the stiff wind.

"You worthless piece of shit! You weren't worth the price of Hider's bullet. Your mother should have drowned you when you were born. I would have held you under with my bare hands until you were blue dead."

Then she fell to her knees weeping and cried out, "Bonner, we got him! Bonner, we got him for you!"

Slocum helped her up and patted her back. "He knows. He knows, Belle."

"Oh, I hope he can hear us, Slocum. I want him so bad to hear me."

So did Slocum.

When the skinning crew returned to their camp and wagons, Hider, as translated by Gloria, told the skinners the story of Bonner's murder. Quickly, everyone began to celebrate the two men's death by dancing and singing. Slocum paid Hider two twenty-dollar gold pieces, and shook his massive calloused hand. Then he and Belle left there.

After sleeping a few hours by themselves out on the prairie, Slocum and Belle headed back to the herd.

"I want to go by and play that piano at Wichita Crossing on our way back," she said. "Somehow, I can get things out of my system like Bonner's death by playing one for a while. It draws the bad things out of me."

"Sure. I'll rent it if need be."

She smiled, rode in close, and slapped his arm. "Why can't I get mad at you? Something about you. I have been mad at every man in my life—sometime. You know, you are damn hard to ever be mad at. Now, who else would have thought about renting a piano so I could play it? I thought you were mad at me anyway. We didn't make love last night."

"No, you fell asleep too soon."

She looked at her hat brim for help, and Slocum would have sworn she blushed.

The sun was low in the west when they reached the crossing. They both dropped heavily from the saddle. Their run-over boot heels stomped across the porch boards, and he held the batwing door open for her. Inside, she swept off her hat, and her long black hair cascaded down on her shoulders.

Some men playing cards looked up. "She's the one who plays the piano," one of them said.

"We ain't *deef*. We heard her the other night."

One tinhorn gambler wearing a stovepipe hat jumped up and bowed. "Ma'am, we'd be honored if you would play for us."

She stopped and looked back at Slocum.

"Floyd?" Slocum called out. "Is that all right with you?"

Floyd stepped up to the bar. "Mrs. Younger, we'd be honored. Play to your heart's content."

She curtsied in her trail-dusty men's clothing and then went to the stool. She set her hat on top of the piano in seconds, her hands tested the keys, and the music began to spill out into the room.

*Rock of ages, cleft for me . . . let me hide myself in thee . . .*

# 14

Next day, when they rode over the last rise, Slocum could see the herd scattered out and grazing. One of the drovers spotted them and came racing to meet them.

Dawson McLain slid his horse on its hind legs. "Did you get 'em?"

Slocum nodded.

Belle gave him a nod, then rode in and slapped him on the arm. "They won't ever kill no more good cowboys. Coalie got anything good to eat left down there?"

"Speaking of him, we're sure glad you're back. Maybe you can get that old coot out of his sour mood."

"Let's do that," she said. "Race you to the wagon."

Slocum shook his head, left to ride into camp alone. She was back to acting like Belle again. Strange how that piano playing drew it out of her—but it sure did wonders. He rode in a jog trot for the wagon.

Belle had filled Coalie in on the whole thing by the time Slocum arrived and dismounted. He dropped the reins and left the horse to graze. Coalie had a cup of steaming coffee poured for him. With a nod, Slocum took the cup and dropped on his haunches beside her.

She held out some dried apple-raisin pie on a fork for him. The sweet treat made his mouth water. "What've you been doing to the boys, Coalie?" he asked.

"Aw, hell, they lounged around like they were unemployed. I told them to get off their asses and be certain there wasn't a herd headed toward us and that all our cattle were staying close."

Slocum grinned. "You did the right thing."

"When we pulling out?" Coalie asked.

"In the morning. We need to get on and see if we can sell these for the top dollar."

"Good, you can roust the boys out now you're here." Grumbling to himself, Coalie went back to his cooking and fire.

"How far away is this place?" Belle asked Slocum.

"Two weeks we should be there."

"Good." She wrinkled her nose. "I'll be ready for civilization."

"There may not be much of that up there."

"We'll see."

He nodded and went for his horse. "I'm going to find Pike and talk to the others."

"Coalie and I'll be here."

He nodded, mounted, and rode off.

Pike came riding in on a hard-trotting horse that looked sweaty. They met a half mile south of camp.

"What do you know?" Slocum asked.

"Guess you found Bonner's killers?"

"They'll not kill anyone else. What's happening?"

Pike gave a head toss to the north. "I've seen several drifting steers wearing a single bar road brand this morning. Can't find the outfit."

"We better split up and see where they are. A few strays is one thing. Several means they're having big problems."

Pike agreed. "They ain't due north. Must be west of the main trail."

"Let's ride."

They took separate high points as much as half a mile apart. Slocum saw several small bunches of unherded cattle wandering as if lost. Then he heard the crack of a pistol shot and could see the gun smoke, and sent his horse north to join Pike.

He headed for the ridge where Pike had turned to go off to the north out of his view. When he crossed the ridge, he could see the wagon and Pike on his knees by someone. He lashed the horse hard with the reins to send him piling down off the slope for the camp.

When he reined up, he could see the grisly scene of dead men and Pike talking to a man he'd propped up against a wagon wheel. The man looked pale as a sheet.

"His name's Jones," said Pike. "He's from west of San Antonio. A gang hit them two nights ago, shot up his crew, and took his remuda and mules. Everyone's dead except him. His name's Clary Jones."

"Clary, can you hear me?" Slocum asked.

The man half opened his eyes and nodded.

"Who owns the cattle?"

"Travis—brothers at San Marcos."

"I'm going to wire them. And hire some help. Did they get all your money?" He'd need some to get this herd on the move again. But he could collect it when the cattle sold if the man was without.

"They got it all," Clary said. "They gunned down the crew like they were shooting hogs."

Slocum nodded. "Can you hang on?"

The cowboy shook his head. "I figure my day's about done. Give them boys a burial—please. I been shooting buzzards. Damn, makes me sick to see them black bastards eating 'em."

"We'll bury 'em."

"Good. I was afraid no one would even come and do that."

"We'll take care of them. Don't worry."

"What do we need to do, Boss?" Pike asked, looking dismayed by the entire situation.

"I'll ride to camp. You stay with him. Belle can ride on to Abilene and she can hire some men who are headed back home to help us bring this herd up there. Or whatever we can find of this herd."

Pike looked pained. "But they don't even have a remuda."

"I'll work on that. I'll bring some of our men back over here to bury them and start rounding up all the cattle we can find."

Pike agreed, and Slocum went for his horse. He took a bottle of whiskey out of his saddlebags and rode over to Pike. "Here, this will ease Jones some."

"Mind if I have a snort?"

Slocum shrugged. "You're in charge."

"Thanks." Pike raised the bottle and toasted him.

Slocum's horse was lathered and done in when he made camp. Belle ran out to meet him. "What did you learn?"

"Some outlaws raided a camp, shot all the cowboys, stole the horses, their money, and left them for the buzzards. Pike's with the only man left alive. He may not make it through the night. I need you to ride to Abilene and wire that man's boss. Tell him we will gather all the cattle that we can find and take them to Abilene.

"Then I want you to find a complete crew, chuck wagon, remuda, and hands that are fixing to go back to Texas. Hire them to gather the cattle and bring them to Abilene, and we'll pay them double wages when the cattle are sold."

"Who do I wire?"

"Travis brothers, San Marcos, Texas. Tell them who we are, tell them we'll bring their money back to a Texas bank or meet them in Fort Worth later. But I want a telegram from them giving me the right to be their agent and sell the cattle."

"I understand. Should I go now?"

He shook his head. "In the morning at first light. Be careful. It must be eighty miles up there. Take two horses and saddle both of them, so you can change animals on the go."

She laughed with excitement. "Darling, I know how to be *careful*. At fifteen, I was running back and forth through those Union lines down in Missouri and Arkansas."

"I bet your daddy wasn't happy about that after all that money he spent on music lessons and schooling."

She wrinkled her nose at him. "No, he wasn't. Quick as he could, he moved my butt to Texas and told me I was to be a lady. Lord sakes, after you've been a spy and running like that delivering messages and telling the Rebs where the Damnyankees were hiding, it was plain boring playing Miss Fluff."

"Besides . . ." She lowered her voice. "I'd learned what boys could do for you and I liked it."

He winked at her. "I see some of the boys are coming in. They need to catch something to eat and get a burying detail together."

"If you go back over there with them, you be sure to wake me up when you get back. I don't want to miss doing it, with me having to leave at dawn for a few days to hire a crew."

"I'll suit your fancy later. Let's go talk to the crew about what they need to do."

After they ate, he and three of the drovers rode back with a shovel and pickax. The rest were on guard duty, even the horse wrangler.

Coalie even offered to help, but Slocum made him stick to camp making fresh coffee and cinnamon-raisin rolls and encouraging the worn-out hands. Belle was helping him, too.

When they got back to the other camp, Slocum saw that Pike had started a mass grave. He looked up, grateful to see them, when they arrived.

"Clary alive?" Slocum asked.

"Barely. I doubt a doctor could help him. But your whis-key made him easier."

"Good. He ever mention anything he saw about those men that would help us find them?"

"They all wore flour-sack masks and long canvas coats. Oh, he said the leader had small silver bells on his spurs. Not jingle bobs. He knew the difference. And that fella also had a sawed-off double-barrel shotgun. That's what he used killing most of the crew."

"He say much more about them?"

"One of those outlaws had consumption. Coughed all the time."

"Not much to go on, is there?"

Pike shook his head, and with a grateful nod began eating off the plate of food that Coalie had sent him. "Been a long, tough day."

"We ain't through either."

Pike looked pained. "I figure two herds to run won't be no piece of cake."

The dead men were buried before the quarter moon rose. Slocum went by and checked on Clary. He was sound asleep, but he was not breathing regular. Slocum would need to bring him some food—Coalie could figure out something. Better get back. Belle would be mad if he didn't wake her for some activity in the bedroll.

He reached down and adjusted his crotch. She'd sure be enough to distract him from all this bloodshed.

Back in camp under a quarter moon, Slocum found their bedroll and Belle over the rise from the chuck wagon. Smil-ing down at her sleeping figure, he nudged her with his boot toe as he undressed.

"Oh . . . you're back." She rustled around under the top cover to get on her back.

When he knelt down, she lifted the cover and he slipped in on top of her warm, naked form. With his hips nested between her spread-out knees, he eased his half-hard dick inside her and she clutched him.

"Darling, I've been dreaming about you."

No matter how tired he felt when climbing in bed with her, she always revived the fires in his flanks. The need to press his charge centered in the cheeks of his butt as he drove in her faster and faster. Her jaw dropped open, and guttural sounds of pleasure escaped her lips. In a dreamy fashion, she tossed her head from side to side, raising her ass to meet his pounding. Her clit stiffened into a nail that tore at the top of his skintight erection.

Then, as if a powerful hand squeezed his balls, two lances pierced his butt, the flood exploded inside her from the swollen hard nose of his cock, and she collapsed.

He eased himself off her and she hugged him. "I'll miss you," she said.

"Be careful. I need you."

"Oh, I will."

He held her tight. There would be challenges ahead to get the other outfit rolling and his own herd up to Abilene as well. He closed his eyes and savored her lithe, warm body pressed to him.

# 15

Slocum knew something was wrong when he arrived at the Travis brothers' camp in the early morning. He dismounted at the chuck wagon.

"Everything all right?" he asked Pike, who was squatted by the wagon, staring off into space.

"Clary Jones died last night."

"Anyone make any breakfast?"

Pike shook his head. "You know, I really got close to him."

"Yes, I know that. What're the boys doing?"

"Hell, Slocum, I don't know. A man works hard. Does his job and then, like Clary, gets killed by some worthless damned outfit. It ain't fair."

"I agree. Is there any firewood?"

"Cow chips, I guess. No wood around here. For two bits, I'd take my horse and go home."

"Pike. Pike, listen to me. I need you—I need you badly. We're almost there. In two weeks it will be over. Don't talk about quitting." Slocum spotted the wood in the cowhide under the wagon's belly. The hands had tried to fill it with dry wood and sticks they found during the day.

"Pike, will you dig him a grave? I'll make some food."

The tall man nodded, but made no move to get up.

Rather than argue with him, Slocum grabbed an ax and attacked the dry wood. He soon had kindling stacked up, enough to start his fire. First, he'd need to boil some water for coffee. He hoped there was some "good" water in the barrel on the side of the wagon. It looked all right coming out of the spigot. When the pot was filled, he set it aside and started the fire. He lit the dry wad of grass with a match and it soon caught his small kindling, and in no time the flames were licking up.

He put the pot on the grill and went for the Dutch oven. It would need hot coals. He'd have some in a while. It looked clean, so he set it aside and went to the fly.

He found the last cook's sourdough liquor. With the lid off he got a quick smell, which assured him the starter should work. The flour bin was full, so he wouldn't have to climb in the wagon and look for more. He ground roasted coffee beans, and soon had enough to make the pot.

He put a huge skillet on the grill to heat. Then, on the countertop under the shade, he began slicing the smoky salt pork side to fry. Coffee, biscuits, and bacon should hold the boys. Where were they? Pike had gone somewhere without a word—maybe to dig the grave?

It would sure be nice to have Belle there to help. She'd probably be more organized than he was about the whole thing. Those boys must be starving. He better get to sorting beans to boil for later.

In a short while, Texas Jim rode in and dismounted. "You're a sight for sore eyes," he said. "My ole belly is eating my backbone."

"Hell, I figured one of you could whip up something to eat." Slocum shook his head in disgust and sliced the sweat off his forehead, bent over, and stoked the fire with more fuel.

"Wasn't a cook among us," Texas Jim said. "I'll chop you some more wood."

"Good, I'll need it. How does the herd look?"

"There's several head in the main bunch. If Belle gets a

crew down here pretty soon, I think we'll have most of them."

Slocum nodded. "You seen Pike? He was here, and next thing I knew he was gone."

"He took Jones's death pretty hard last night."

Slocum nodded and straightened up. He put his hands on his hips, and the ache in the center of his lower back made him wince. "We still have to go on."

Texas Jim agreed. "This smoke should bring them in. I caught a whiff of it and said either Coalie's up there or a miracle's happening."

Slocum nodded and poured the ground coffee into the pot. "We'll at least have coffee shortly. You never appreciate a cook till you don't have one."

"Amen to that. Rube and Harvey are coming in."

"I see them. Where in the hell did Pike go?"

Texas Jim shook his head. "I'll go find him."

"Do that."

Slocum was busy making dough, satisfied he'd soon have enough hot coals to heat the Dutch oven. He poured some of the liquor into the flour and went to mixing. It had been a while since he'd made any bread, so he hoped this worked.

Then a shot rang out. He put down the broad scraping tool he was using to mix the ingredients. and went to check it out. What had happened now? On the rise, he saw Texas Jim returning and waving for him to stay where he was.

"What happened?" Slocum asked as Texas Jim drew closer.

"I guess Jones's death and all was more than Pike could stand." Then Texas Jim stopped, bent over, and puked. Shaking his head, he held his hand out for Slocum to give him a minute.

At last, he managed to say, "Before I could stop him, he committed suicide."

What else would happen? Maybe Norm Ryder had seen a weakness in Pike. That was why he hadn't made Pike the trail boss when Schmid was killed in Fort Worth. Slocum turned away and fought down the sourness rising in his own throat. Damn.

Later on, the drovers gathered in camp. Slocum's biscuits hardly made the grade, but the men ate them when they were done. They chewed on his fried salt pork. Texas Jim, Rube, Harvey, and Slocum ate in silence.

Slocum checked the sun time. Near midday. His beans were boiling in the kettle. Maybe they'd get done by sundown. Three cowboys came by while they were eating. They looked hungover, but they also looked like a gift from heaven to Slocum.

"Heading home?" Slocum asked.

The oldest, a freckle-faced youth of perhaps eighteen, nodded, looking like the spokesman for the three. "Yes, mister, if this is the way back to San Antonio."

"Climb down, men. I have a proposition. The drovers on this drive were robbed and murdered a few nights ago. I'm trying to round up their cattle and get them on to Abilene. I'll pay you boys fifty a month to help gather the cattle, and then I'll feed you all the way back home."

The three searched each other's faces; then the leader stepped down. "You've got yourself a deal, mister. My name's Shawn Hyde, that's the Kid and Blackie Crane. We were serious wondering how we'd eat going home."

The Kid wrestled up his pants with one hand and said, "We're damn sure tired of eating rabbits we been shooting for meals."

"I've got some sorry biscuits, but they'll have to do for now. We'll go get you some fresh horses from our other remuda. Texas Jim here will be the boss until we get going. I have more help coming."

The new cowboys acted grateful for the coffee, bacon, and the biscuits. There was still plenty of fried pork left, and they ate while talking about how they lost their money in dishonest card games. They even blushed when Harvey asked if they'd gotten any pussy.

"One that I had was so ugly, her mother wouldn't have kissed her." The Kid dropped his gaze to the ground in defeat. "Damn strange how you can yearn so hard to do something like that and when you get some, it's a stinking, sloppy mess."

"Ah," Rube said. "You just got a bad apple out of a barrel. Did you pick her?"

"Hell, no. I stood in line for over an hour, and finally this old gal grabbed my arm and hauled me down the hall to this room. Made me pay her fifteen bucks, and then she smiled and with a shove, pushed me into the room. 'Fuck her good, sonny boy,' she said, and slammed the door after me. Hell, a damn sheep would have beat that bitch in bed."

They all laughed.

Fifteen bucks for a piece of ass? Slocum shook his head over the inflated price as he went around refilling coffee cups.

"What's the name of this outfit?" Shawn asked.

"It belongs to the Travis brothers."

Blackie Crane grinned big. "I know them sonsabitches. They wouldn't hire me for this drive. Said I was just a boy. Billy Raymond didn't say that. He hired me."

"But he never offered to feed you going home either, did he?" Slocum asked.

"No, sir, and I'm plumb grateful for you doing that."

Slocum laughed. "Me and the Travis brothers. Boys, the day's passing fast and we need to dig a grave. One of our main men couldn't take it any more . . . he shot himself this morning."

They buried Pike. Slocum said a few words, and Texas Jim took the three new hands around to show them the cattle and what they were doing. The beans would be edible by evening, and he left Harvey in charge of feeding everyone while he and Rube went for some remuda horses to get things rolling.

His own herd looked contented enough when they rode past. Coalie came out to meet them.

"How's it going, Boss Man?"

"Not good. Pike shot himself this morning. Guess it all got to him."

Coalie chewed his lower lip and part of the bushy beard as well. "Shame. He was a good man."

"He have any kin we know about?"

Coalie shook his head. "Come to think of it, I never heard him say."

"I don't think he did," Rube said as Coalie filled their cups with steaming coffee.

"Well, I hired three riders today. That will help. I hope Belle finds us a crew up there and quick. I guess we better go back in the morning. I don't think any of them cook, and we need to take some horses from our remuda for them."

Coalie agreed "The boys are easing these cattle north to keep them in good grass. I may move tomorrow."

"Fine. We ever get two crews, we can roll again."

"Yeah, one's tough enough," Rube said, and took off his hat to scratch the top of his head. "But we'll do it."

Slocum blew on his coffee. Still hot as fire. But it was a damn sight better'n his own.

The next morning, Slocum and Rube took the horses cut out of the remuda over to the other camp. The cowboys had reheated beans and coffee, and were glad to see the fresh ponies. Ropes whirled, and soon they were mounted up. Texas Jim took charge of the riders, and they rode out while Rube and Slocum worked on the next meal.

"I never realized Coalie did this much work," Rube said with an armload of firewood for the stack. "He needs a helper."

"Didn't want one, he told me," Slocum said. "They got in his way."

"Well—" Free of his load, Rube stretched his back. "This is a tough job."

"How did a Jewish boy ever become a cowboy?"

"I never liked stitching clothes. My people in Georgia were tailors. War got over, I simply headed West. I'd been in cavalry during the war so I could ride a horse. Ryder hired me and I've been a cowboy ever since."

"No problem. Just curious."

"I'm going to have a ranch of my own someday."

"I bet you have a good one."

Rube nodded. "It will be."

"Those boys will have beans again today. Go to sorting them. It beats rabbits anyway."

"Tell me about the missus if you want to."

"Belle Younger. That's her name. She had a baby by Cole Younger, I guess. Claims they were married. He rode off. She's highly educated and likes adventures."

"Where is the baby?"

"Her aunt has it."

Rube sat down on his butt and sipped the coffee. "What will happen? I mean to her."

Slocum joined him. "Damned if I know. I had a crippled horse in Arkansas. She stopped and befriended me. The law must have been following her all along looking for Cole. They thought I was him."

"What did you do?"

"We ran away."

Rube laughed. "I would, too, if she'd gone with me."

"She's all right. But man, she can get mad."

Rube nodded.

That evening back at camp, Slocum stood beyond the firelight and listened to the coyotes yip at the moon rising in the east. A million stars pricked the sky, and the heat of the day had begun to evaporate.

Two days hard ride up there, two days waiting on a return telegram from the Travis brothers, hiring new crew, and then Belle should be headed back. He couldn't get over the Kid's story about his experience with that whore and spending a half month's wages for some dove that would have done it for two bits out back.

*Come home . . . Belle . . . I miss you.*

# 16

His new crew was gathering Travis cattle. Slocum began to believe that the cattle weren't all as badly scattered as he'd originally thought. The herd grew each day. He dropped in and did some cooking so they'd have food. Texas Jim was doing a great job and the three boys rode hard for him. Rube kept things up, like saddle repairs, and looked after the horses as well as making rides around the herd to keep them in a loose bunch.

He also oversaw the feeding of the men.

"They complain about our food yet?" Slocum asked.

"No, they ain't forgot eating rabbit yet."

"Well, you've got enough bread made and beans cooking. Watch it don't scorch. I'm going over to our camp."

"No sign of the missus?" Texas Jim asked.

"She'll be coming back soon." Or he'd go see about her. He was close to getting edgy about her not returning.

"I hope so. This job as camp cook and horse wrangler and the rest is a hard business."

Later, back at his own outfit, Slocum looked up. There was a rider coming out of the north. Riding a horse and leading one—Belle was coming back.

He swept off his hat for her, and she slid to halt in a cloud of dust. When it settled, she was off her horse, in his arms, kissing him like they'd been apart for years.

"Whew." She pushed her hat back on her shoulders, and her black hair spilled out. From her vest she handed him a yellow telegram.

MUCH THANKS, MR. SLOCUM    YOU ARE
OUR AGENT TO MAKE ANY DEAL
NECESSARY    ONE OF US WILL MEET YOU IN
FORT WORTH TO SETTLE WITH YOU    THIS
WAS A VERY GENEROUS OFFER    GOD BLESS
YOU AND YOUR MEN    VERNON TRAVIS

"Is there a crew coming?" Slocum asked.

"Yes, and he has a good remuda. He has a cook and ten hands. His name is Victor Cross. He's from the hill country— Bernie. I said fifty a month for the hands, hundred for him, and we'd foot the supplies."

Slocum hugged her. "He's on his way?"

"Said he'd be here in a few days."

"Damn, that's news worth celebrating," Coalie said, and danced a jig. "You can play Harvey's fiddle over that. I'll get it out of the wagon."

"What do you think?" she asked as if struck by the notion.

"Play it."

In no time at all, her fiddle music brought in every hand. Slocum broke out a bottle of good whiskey to celebrate, and the crew was individually dancing in the dirt to the Virginia waltz. Holding their tin cups high, the drovers were putting on a show. And she intently sawed away on the fiddle as though playing it was an obligation.

Slocum exhaled. One battle won. Two more to go. Get his own crew back and rolling, then get this Victor Cross and his bunch trailing in the Travis herd. And maybe he could have Belle in his bedroll and fiddle around with her.

Deep in his throat, he chuckled over the notion of having

her supple body again before he took another swallow of the smooth whiskey. And the herd'd be on the road in a few days—headed north.

Victor Cross was the broadest-chested man Slocum had ever met. Maybe six feet seven, the man would have needed an entire buggy seat to himself. His blue eyes twinkled and he stuck out a calloused hand to shake.

"The little woman said you'd inherited a peck of trouble."

Slocum agreed, and invited the man over to the campfire for coffee. "A gang of outlaws struck, murdered the men, took all their money, stole the mules and horses. The foreman lived a few days, but he was bad shot up and we lost him. I have their permission to be their agent and sell the herd."

"Good. The boys and I can use the work." Victor laughed. "Most of them already spent all they made, and my boss will sure appreciate you going their board for the trip home. Lots of outfits put those boys on their own. It's a damn long way back to Texas without any money."

"Yes, it is. I hired three young drovers that were eating rabbits and headed home. They can help you."

"Sure. What's the plan?"

"First, I need someone to take their wagon back to Wichita Crossing and park it there with the store man. He'll watch it. I'll buy a team in Abilene to take it back and we can drive it to Texas on our return. It's a new wagon and no use letting someone steal it."

"Right. One of my crew can take my mules and move it down there while we're getting things settled for the drive."

"Good. Those boys have rounded up lots of those cattle. We can't get them all, but let's say we spend three days looking for any others. Fourth day, you head them for Abilene. I'll be a day ahead of you with my herd."

"Sounds good. Now how far away is that other herd?"

"I'll show you. It's about five miles over there. I been watching so no herds collide with either of them. It's a good thing it's late in the season or we'd've been overrun."

"Good idea."

"I'll cinch up my horse and take you over there."

"Meet my boys first," Cross said. "I told them they'd get at least a month's pay, right?"

"I'll sure do that."

He went down the line and shook hands with Cross's crew standing beside their horses. Big Jake, Little Jake, Thomas, Old Tom, Rad, Booger, Snake-eyes, Helm, Walsh, and Goody the cook.

"Nice to have you boys. Keep your guns handy. All I know about the outlaws is one of the killers had a pair of spurs with tiny silver bells, not jingle bobs."

"Mr. Slocum, sir," the youth called Helm said. "I seed a man in Abilene had them kinda spurs."

"Drover?"

Helm shook his head and curled his lip. "He was dressed more like a gambler."

"Catch his name?"

"Maybe it was Booth?"

"Thanks, I'll check that out." The killer might still be in the area. "We get you up there and you see him, you come find me. It might be a coincidence, but a dying man mentioned that kinda spur."

Belle rode in and dismounted. She waved and smiled at the crew, leading her horse over to join Slocum. Each man swept off his hat for her when she went by them.

"Good looking bunch, aren't they?" She beamed at them.

"Real handsome crew," Slocum said. "We're going over to the Travis herd right now."

"I'll ride along," she said, and vaulted back in the saddle.

Near sundown, they approached the campfire. Texas Jim came out to meet them.

After introductions, they sat by the campfire while Goody boiled up some real coffee and Belle served it, flirting with the crew as she went about filling their cups.

Texas Jim agreed to stay two more days with them before he went back to the Ryder herd. Shawn, who had ridden point for his past employer, was going over to take Pike's place. The other two hands with Shawn agreed to help Cross get that herd to Abilene.

When all that was settled, Slocum and Belle headed back for their herd. The crickets' and locusts' symphony filled the warm night. Riding stirrup to stirrup, they jog-trotted their horses eastward across the rolling grassland.

"You know what I'd like to do?" she said.

"No. What's that?"

"I'd like to stop and find a place to roll out your ground cloth and see how many times you and I can do it."

"How many times we can—"

"You heard me."

"You pick the place, lady."

"How about right here?"

He reined up his horse. "Good enough."

"I can tell you the most horrible thing happened in the middle of that trip to Abilene."

"What was that?"

"I had my—time."

"Oh?"

"There I was with nothing and I needed to go on. I finally got to Abilene and found me a house and they fixed me up."

"Lucky you've got friends in such places." Amused, he shook his head at her. "You should have heard the Kid's story about losing his virginity after standing in line forever, paying fifteen dollars, and being shoved in a room with one he said was so ugly he couldn't describe her."

"Oh, my goodness, that would be enough to turn any man off women." She was wiggling the britches off her slender hips. Then, she shed her vest and her shirt. "You know, I really missed you."

"I missed you. We've kinda become a team."

She dropped to her knees on the canvas sheet and waded over in front of him. "Well, get ready. This game is about to begin."

With her right hand, she caught his cock in her fist and began kissing the head of it. When it emerged like a flower on a stem, she leaned back and laughed. "You are the horniest man in Kansas."

"Hell, how do you know? You ain't seen them all." He tousled her thick hair with both hands.

"Shit, I know, trust me."

"All right, get on your back and we'll see if I am or not."

She put her hands behind her so she could shake her tits at him. "I'll be so damn sore in the morning I'll have to ride 'cause I won't be able to walk."

"I hope so."

He moved her down on her back until he replaced his finger with his tool. He poked his throbbing dick in her wet cunt. She gasped for breath. "Wonderful. Wonderful. God, Slocum, I missed you."

If there ever was a bitch mink in heat, Belle had to be the hottest one. Her wild antics underneath him made his head whirl. He probed her as hard and deep as he could, her bare heels spurring him on like he was a racehorse. With his hands, he clasped the rock-hard halves of her ass to get as deep inside her as he could. The walls of her pussy's spasmodic muscles closed like a slamming door and he had to repenetrate her each time with much effort.

Their breath raged in their throats. His chest ached. His back felt broken. Then a cramp in his balls sent a message the time was close, and he came twice inside her.

She fainted, sprawled on her back in the starlight, her bare arms askew and her eyes shut. Braced above her, he laughed.

"What's—so—funny. . . . Damn—I must have. . . ." Then she fell asleep.

"Nothing, love, nothing. I think you did yourself in."

Before sunrise, they were on their way to camp, riding side by side under a half-moon.

"Damn you, Slocum. Where will you go when we sell these cattle?"

"I don't know, Belle. I've got some wanted posters on my ass. They're federal and every once in a while I draw a Pinkerton man or some bounty hunter."

"Come on down to Younger's Bend country. We'll look out for you down there."

"Belle, I get restless. I don't want to be a dirt farmer."

"Suit yourself, but I bet you don't find another woman as well suited as I am to you."

He nodded. "I never said I would."

She swatted him on the forearm with her quirt. "By Gawd, you won't either."

Then she angrily raced off and left him. He shrugged and rode on in a short lope. Belle might be the sexiest woman in the land, but she also was the hardest to please. Damn her hide. He ought to bend her over his knees and bust her ass with that damn crop.

Maybe if her old daddy had done that a few times with her growing up, she'd've made a real wife for someone. Half mad at her actions, he sent the bay after her. He might just be the one to set her straight. In a short while, he drew the gelding down to a jog trot. Hell with her.

When he reached camp, the sun was coming up and Coalie was ringing the triangle.

"What did you do to make her so gawdamn mad?" Coalie asked when Slocum walked up.

"Why?"

"She flew in her, got her bags, tied them on her saddle, and left cussing me like a sailor."

"Hard to keep that woman pleased." Slocum went on for some coffee. She had gotten mad and cut out. This drive was about over anyway. Hell, he sure wasn't going to marry her. Cole had already tried that, or so she said.

Blowing on the steaming cup, he watched the boys selecting their horses and getting ready for the day. He might take a few riders and make a wide circle to see if there were any more strays they could round up.

He accepted a heaping plate of side meat, fried potatoes

and onions, biscuits and gravy, and some grits. Given the fact that he couldn't recall the last time he'd eaten, he sat down cross-legged and joined with the punchers.

"Who set Miss Belle on fire?" Rube asked. "She cleared this place like she was pissed at the whole world."

"Guess I did. It ain't hard to make that woman mad." Slocum made a big circle with his fork. "She's off to do her things, I reckon."

They all chuckled.

"She ain't coming back?" Blister asked.

"Now, if I knew that, hoss, I'd be about the smartest man on this earth," Slocum said, savoring a mouthful of Coalie's good grub.

After the meal, he and four of the hands rode out to scout for stock. Making a big swing east, they covered lots of country and only found a dozen or so steers with the Travis brand. McLain came back to join the bunch about noon.

"I found maybe a hundred head, but the fella that's got them ain't going to release 'em."

"Who is he?"

"Calls himself Hardy. Randy Hardy."

"How far away is he?" Slocum asked as they all gathered in with the few head of steers they'd found.

McLain pointed to the northeast.

Slocum nodded. "Blister, you keep this bunch here. We'll go see what this man's deal is."

In a short while, they crossed a ridge, and the smoke from the tin pipe on the soddy roof bent in the strong wind. McLain pointed out the cattle.

"Why, he ain't even got a crop out," Slocum said, thinking the man wanted to be paid for damage to his corn crop.

A hatless whiskered man with a long muzzle-loading rifle came outside and looked in their direction. Who in the hell did he think he was? Slocum leaned back and unlimbered a .50-caliber Spencer from his scabbard. He never left camp anymore without one.

"Spread out, boys. We don't want trouble, but we may get some."

Solemn nods came from his men as they obeyed his order.

"That's close enough," the man shouted. "I told that sumbitch works for you that you weren't getting them cows back. It's finders keepers, losers weepers around here."

"Hardy. Those steers belong to the Travis brothers in San Marcos, Texas, and I'm their agent," Slocum shouted. "We come to get them. I'd pay you a reward for your troubles, but I ain't buying this crap about you keeping them. But there ain't no need in anyone dying over a hundred head of cattle."

"Well, you ride in closer and you'll all die."

"Ain't the way I want it, Hardy. You better think long and hard about this. Those are branded cattle and they belong to the brand owner." Time to settle this standoff. He booted his horse toward the house.

"I said—" Hardy drew the carbine to his shoulder as Slocum took aim with his Spencer.

Smoke from Hardy's carbine looked like white flour. The black gun smoke from Slocum's Spencer blew quickly away, and the man lay on the ground in front of the soddy. Slocum levered in a fresh round.

"Gather those cattle, boys. Daylight's burning."

Grim-faced, McLain nodded. "I knew he was dead set on keeping them. But I sure didn't figure he'd die over 'em."

Slocum shook his head. He'd given the man a choice. Hardy had simply taken the wrong option. Better go down there and see about his people. If he had any.

A teenage girl was on her knees over the still body when he dismounted. Dressed in rags and with long stringy hair in her face, she tried to fight it but looked ready to cry. "You done kilt him, mister."

Slocum nodded. "I made him a good offer. He was stupid to shoot at us."

Tears streamed down her face. "What'll I do now?"

"He your pa?"

"Naw. I's his woman. Sadie." She indicated Hardy.

"You're a mite young to be his wife, ain't ya?"

She shrugged. "Pa traded me to him."

Slocum frowned. "What for?"

"Some food, flour, and the like so him, Ma, and the others could get to Orie-gon."

"You better find a shovel. We'll bury him."

"What'll I do? Where will I go? I ain't got anyone now."

Slocum looked at the sun time. Near noon. Damn, he had another orphan and a grave to dig. "Harvey, you stay here and help me plant him. Rest of you boys head those cattle to the Travis herd. Tell Victor I'll check with him in the morning."

He turned to the girl. "Pack your things. We'll take you with us."

She clenched her fists and screamed at him, "To where?"

Slocum shook his head. "Abilene." He could see she was about to go over the edge.

Then she fainted.

He saw the smirk on McLain's face when he turned his horse away to follow the others after the livestock. Might as well have said, *What do you do now, Boss Man?*

Harvey found the shovel and began cutting squares out of the sod to start the grave. When the handle cracked, in his anger, the disgusted Slocum slung his hat on the ground, ready to stomp it.

"I'm sorry—"

"Hell, Harvey, I never said you did it. We need to drag his body inside. And shut the door. And come back tomorrow with a good shovel and bury him."

Harvey agreed.

"I don't think she has much stuff," Slocum said. "You can haul her back to our camp. I'll go ride over there with the crew and the cattle. Let's get his body inside. Damn."

Slocum closed his eyes. What could go wrong next?

# 17

It was past sundown when Slocum and the boys made it back to their own camp. Coalie stood up, wiping his hands on his apron, to greet them.

"Old Harve made it in with Sadie." Coalie grinned. "First time he's been that close to a woman, I figure, in his life." The cook snickered. "She had her arms tied around him tighter than a cinch on a bronc all the way for fear she'd fall off. Why, he was so red-faced over it, I thought he'd bust open when he got back here."

"Some of us have to go back and bury Hardy tomorrow."

"No, Rube and Harvey went back to do it tonight."

"Where's she at?" Slocum spun around to look for her.

"Who's that, Sadie or Belle?"

Slocum frowned.

"Yeah, she come back, too. Why, Belle took one look at that filthy girl and drug her off for a bath and to put some different clothes on her."

"Sounds like Belle."

"Oh, yeah. We've got some beef tonight. We slaughtered one of those strays today. Figured you could take the other outfit half of it. Keep the canvas wrap wet, it'll keep for several days."

"Great idea."

"How's she look?" Belle asked, dragging the girl by the arm.

Head down, embarrassed by all the attention, the girl wouldn't look up at them. But her formerly greasy hair looked new, and the dress was a little large, but out of the rags and washed up, she looked human enough.

"Better eat, Sadie. Coalie's got some fine food," Slocum said with his plate full of chunks of beef in a rich gravy.

"Mr. Slocum—thank—you."

"No, just be one of us, girl. We're just a crew of cowboys trying to get done here."

She nodded, and Belle guided her to the side bar on the chuck wagon, but not before giving Slocum a small kick in the leg going past. What the hell had he done to deserve that? It was Belle who'd gone off in a huff for no reason he'd figured out.

Two hours later in the bedroll, acting like nothing had ever happened between them, she snuggled underneath him ready to begin. She pulled his face down to kiss her, and then giggled. "If you could have heard that child's stories about her short life with that crazy man, you would laugh, too."

"Who trades his own daughter for a barrel of flour and goods anyway?"

"Oh, yes, her father must have been a winner, too. You know, there were lots of folks before and during the war in Arkansas and Missouri that poor. I knew a man who brought his own wife to this officer and offered to trade her services for food. I saw her later in Dallas working in a whorehouse. I asked her where her old man was at. She laughed and said who knew where he was at. She wasn't feeding him anymore."

And then Slocum entered her and they plunged into lovemaking.

Dawn came. He was up and moving and began going over his mental list. They needed to examine saddles and girths, grease the chuck wagon wheels, and be ready to roll the next morning. Send half the beef to Victor, who was shaping up the other herd. Be lucky if they weren't short five hundred head when they finally got them to Abilene, but those brothers would have had nothing if Slocum and his crew hadn't stepped in to help.

Pike's suicide needled him. Good man. No telling what he was thinking or why he'd killed himself. His life had become too crowded for him to survive in it. The steam off the coffee softened the whiskers around Slocum's mouth. No telling.

"You look filled up with serious things this morning," Belle said when she joined him as he sat on the ground with his plate of food.

"We roll out tomorrow. In less than a week, we'll be in Abilene."

"So that's what we came for. Deliver this herd, and then the herd of the Travis brothers, too. You've not done bad." She went to eating.

"I don't mean that. I'd like to find the men that raided that herd and stole the horses and everything else."

She dinged her fork on his plate to get his attention. "We'll find them. There is not much you and I can't do together. Since we left Coal Hill, Arkansas, in the middle of the night, I knew I had joined a real man."

He lowered his voice. "Why did you run out mad?"

"Ah, I have fits once in a while that I cannot control."

He nodded. At least, she realized she had them—she called them fits. Strange woman, but he loved having her around. Made his life a lot more interesting.

"Where is your girl?" he asked.

"Helping Coalie. She's making some fried pies, I think. Poor girl is bashful as all get out, and she don't know much about anything. I asked her if she was pregnant, and she looked at me like, what is that?"

"Is she?"

"I don't think so. If she is, we'll have some doctor restart her. She's too young, no husband, and she does not need a baby."

Slocum nodded. "I guess you're right."

Looking satisfied, Belle nodded. "I know."

"I'm going over to the other herd and be sure they are all set. You wish to ride over there today?"

"I think so."

"Fine. I need the boys to check on everything today so we're ready to roll at dawn."

"Abilene, here we come ready or not."

Slocum nodded, and held out his cup for Coalie to refill from the big pot he carried around. "How's your new helper?" he asked the cook.

"Why, she's handy as a pocket on a shirt. We'll be having fried pies here in a moment."

"Good." Slocum winked at Belle.

She nodded.

At mid-morning, the two of them found Victor in the other camp. Some of his men were sleeping. No doubt, after a night of herding and getting ready to leave, they could stand the rest.

"Any notion on how many cattle we have to take to Abilene?" Slocum asked.

"We've been making some counts when they were spread out grazing. I'd say around fifteen hundred head."

Slocum nodded. "I am guessing, but most herds this size are around two thousand head when they start, so that many shouldn't be a disaster for the brothers. Folks have lost all their cattle in stampedes, in river crossings, and rustling even. I bet they're sitting on cactus down there wondering if they'll even have any money when this is over."

Victor agreed.

"Tell me about this woman who rides with you," Victor said, watching Belle converse with his cook over by the chuck wagon. "She would be a very lovely woman in a dress, no?"

"She is lovely in a dress. I met her in Arkansas. My horse went lame. She offered me a ride in a buggy. Told me she was Cole Younger's wife."

"Isn't he riding with Jesse James?"

"Vic, you know as much as I do."

"My, my, what a windfall for you, my man. We all sleep with our fist. You have the lovely lady."

"'Cause I'm the boss."

Victor laughed harder before he quit. "Yes, and I have had fun gathering this herd besides having my board paid home."

"Good enough. My outfit'll leave in the morning."

"We'll be on your heels the next day."

"Be careful. There's more outlaws out there between here and there."

"My men are all armed."

Slocum nodded. "Since you've been to Abilene, tell me what I'll face. This business of cattle dealers, commission men. What do you suggest?"

"Man, it's sure not easy. They're like buffalo gnats. They'll swarm you. A fella I traded with named McClanahan was the best one I found. But you sure need to know the market. They're all crooks in my book. They buy low, sell high."

"I thought they were commission men and would get the most for you so they got a higher commission."

"All I can say is watch yourself."

"Thanks for the advice." Slocum nodded. "Tell the crew to enjoy that beef. You and me'll toss down some good whiskey in Abilene when this booger is over."

"Oh, they'll enjoy it all right. See you up the road. Good luck making your sale." Victor smiled. Slocum knew the man was jealous about his and Belle's relationship, but in a friendly way.

"McClanahan is his name?"

"He has a shack near the cattle shipping pens. But his money was good."

"Thanks."

Slocum's business completed, he and Belle rode back to their place. The trip proved uneventful, and he found the men lounging around getting rested for the next day. Slocum felt like he'd forgotten something, but couldn't remember what it could have been. His conscience jabbed him all day, but by sundown he decided he was simply overly worried about moving again and finding a good buyer.

In the predawn, the camp boiled with activity, drovers catching horses, then dragging their tied-up bedrolls to the wagon and stacking them for Coalie to load. There was electricity in the air. Slocum was giving assignments, and lots of laughing and teasing was going on.

Sadie was going to ride with Coalie in the wagon. In an apron that about swallowed her, she dished out food to the boys, blushing at their thank-yous.

"Poor girl's going to have a new complexion," Slocum said, sitting down with his plate in one hand and coffee in the other.

"What's that?" Belle asked beside him.

"Red from blushing."

"Aw, she's twice as brave today as yesterday."

"She's fine. You ready for Abilene?" he asked Belle.

"I been there once. Remember, you sent me up there?"

"Well, you ready for another dose?"

"No." She lowered her voice. "Am I losing you there?"

"I plan to go back to Texas and deliver the money to the owners."

"Good," she said as if satisfied, and went to eating.

The steers were hard to get up, but finally they began to rise and stretch their backs. With his point men in place, the herd began to file northward. Drovers shouting, a few whips cracking, cattle bawling for some buddy they lost, a few fights over who's in charge, and they were off like a well-oiled machine.

Slocum was riding his horse in a slow lope, tricking errant steers back to the herd, waving in approval to his hands when he saw them doing the same thing. They rolled north for the rail sidings and an end to the drive.

The sixth day, Slocum and Belle rode into Abilene to see about a buyer. Several cattle buyers had been by the herd in the past two days, but Slocum felt they were all low bidders. They talked about a slow market, that the cattle were worth maybe six cents a pound. He felt certain it was mostly scare tactics so they could buy the cattle cheap and make a large profit.

What did he know about the market after being on the trail for a couple of months? There were shysters all over, especially when it came to the amount of money two thousand head would bring.

Finally, at his small office, Slocum met Duart McClanahan, a short Scotsman in his forties who reached over a desk piled high with papers and receipts to shake his hand. Then Slocum introduced Belle.

"Nice to meet you, ma'am.

"What have ya got, me laddie?"

"A man named Victor Cross said he dealt with you. I have near two thousand three-year-olds. All steers. No scrubs. Top cattle."

"Yes, yes, I did business with Victor Cross. Big man. How far away are they?"

"Be a day's ride south tomorrow. What do you pay?"

"Ah, let's see." McClanahan began digging through his papers. "Oh, around seven cents a pound."

Slocum shook his head in disgust. "I've been offered a better price than that from a buyer who was at my herd yesterday."

The man stopped shifting papers and looked hard at Slocum. "What did he offer?"

"Nine cents a pound."

"That's outrageous. We haven't paid that high an amount per pound in months."

"Guess we better go on, Belle," Slocum said.

"Don't be foolish. Wait. I have railcars. I can get you cash on the barrelhead. Say nine cents."

"I didn't take his offer 'cause I figure that fella out there was five cents too cheap."

"Oh, no, laddie, ten cents is the best offer you'll be getting in this burg."

"I have another herd coming behind this one."

"Same owner?"

"No, but I'm the agent. The crew was murdered by robbers and the horses taken. I am the agent for them. I have a telegram to prove it."

"Aw, we've heard about such rascals. I'll look at your first herd and if I can—if I can, offer you the very top price. Can we have them here in two days? The demurrage on those cars is expensive."

"You want to go see them in the morning?"

"No, this afternoon—right now."

Slocum wondered about the man's haste. Was it the cost per day of the cars sitting on the siding, or was this man really needing cattle for a shipment? It looked like there was no shortage of cattle. They'd passed several herds on their way into town.

"I'll go get my horse. We can go now." McClanahan put on his derby hat and green checkered coat.

Outside, Slocum whispered in Belle's ear. "You stay here in town. Find out for me the going price for cattle. I'll ride out and show him the steers. Meet you here when we get back late this evening."

She agreed. "He sure acts strange, don't he."

"I don't care how he acts. I want my money and the best price I can get."

"Sure, I know that." She gave him her broad smile. "Darling, I will know the market backward and forward by the time you get back, I promise you."

"She's not going with us?" The cattle buyer looked disappointed at this.

"You know women." Slocum reined his horse around to go back south. "She's got business here in town."

"Oh, women, yes. Let's ride."

On the way, McClanahan spoke about the railhead problems, the slaughter market in Chicago, developing his own buying operation, and other topics. In fact, by the time they located his herd, Slocum felt he knew everything about cattle marketing.

McClanahan was no stranger to Texas cattle, and they rode slowly through the grazing herd in the twilight. The man under the derby looked them over closely.

At last, he spoke. "Good big-framed cattle. You could feed them corn for a few months, they'll hang on some weight. I can use them. I'll pay you ten cents a pound but I want an extra three-percent cut for the bad ones."

"You asking that sixty head be given to you as compensation for bad ones?" Slocum looked at the man in disbelief.

"That's standard. Many herds, I ask for more than that."

"When I took on this job, the man said my pay depended on how many steers I could get to Abilene. I ain't lost sixty steers since I left Fort Worth. I'll be damned if I'd flat give you sixty head for being a commission man."

"You don't understand."

"I understand you are asking for five thousand dollars to make this deal."

"Well, not that much—"

"I went to school. I can figure that real quick. You're making a profit off me and one off that farmer over there that's going to feed them. No, I'm not giving a three-percent cut."

"You don't understand."

"McClanahan, you are not talking to some old boy came in here barefooted. I'm ready to head back to Abilene."

"I have expenses—"

"Man that owns them has expenses, too."

"You mean you won't sell them to me?" The man looked aghast.

"I'll let you know when we get to Abilene. Tell me your best offer."

The cattle buyer made a face and then, like he was pulling teeth, said, "Eleven cents a pound and one-percent cut."

"I'll let you know in Abilene."

"Why not now?"

"'Cause my lady is checking prices for me."

"She—she won't beat that."

"She does, you don't get the cattle."

It was long after sundown when they returned to town. Darkness had swallowed the town, save for the lights on in the roaring saloons that could be seen in the street.

"What's that hymn?" McClanahan asked. "Who's playing a hymn?"

Slocum knew, and she had gathered a large audience. A lady named Belle Younger, and the refrains of her hymn rolled out in the dusty street. The overflow crowd outside on the boardwalk was singing it and some of them were crying.

*Rock of Ages cleft for me, let me hide myself in thee . . .*

# 18

Slocum made his way inside the packed saloon. To maneuver through the whores, drunken cowboys, buckskin freighters, and tinhorn gamblers was no small task, but he was patient. He soon joined Belle on the bench as she swayed like a willow tree in the wind tinkling the ivories.

"Have a nice ride?" she asked.

"Eleven cents a pound and one percent cut."

Grinning, she looked up at the tin ceiling squares, acting pleased with his words. "Oh, you have done very well."

"Good." He relaxed a little. "Your music is wonderful and your audience is charmed."

"Then kiss me on the mouth in approval."

His eyes narrowed. Was she serious? "You going to stop playing?"

"No."

"All right." He kissed her hard and the crowd gave a cheer. Belle never missed a note. "I need to go tell McClanahan I'll take it. He'll be sending a boy to tell Coalie we need to start with five hundred head cut out and drove in here in two days."

She nodded, intent on playing a new selection, "Turkey

in the Straw." "Do they have a honeymoon suite in that hotel down the street?" she asked.

"I'll see. How long are you going to play here?"

"Until you come back for me."

He looked over the attentive faces that surrounded them. The people were all clapping and stomping to the music. Not hardly a dry eye in the crowd.

"I'll be back in thirty minutes or so."

"Wonderful, my darling. Simply wonderful. I can't wait."

Once outside, he told McClanahan they had a deal and shook on it.

The man looked relieved. "I'll send that boy to tell your man how to send the cattle in and that you'll meet them. Is that really your woman in there playing?"

"I'm with her." Slocum smiled at the man. Cattle deal closed. Next, he needed a room—a honeymoon suite, she said.

In the Cattleman's Cottage Hotel, the clerk told him the honeymoon suite was twenty dollars a night and waited for him to blow up at the price.

"I want it for a week."

The young clerk blinked and swallowed hard. "You Texans are sure doers."

"We are?" Slocum laughed.

"That's a hundred and forty dollars. Yes, you fellas sure are doers."

"I've spent more than that on a lot less. Draw up two hot baths in thirty minutes and have them in the room."

"That's extra."

"I said—"

"Yes, sir."

"Are there any roses in Abilene?"

The boy nodded sharply. "I can find some—sir."

"I'd like some."

"They will be in your room."

"What is your name?"

"Elmer, sir. Elmer Layton."

"Elmer, here's a silver dollar. That's yours for being such a great clerk."

"Yes, sir. I'll have it all up there when you get back—Mr.—Mr. Slocum."

Slocum left his horse with a livery man, slung his saddlebags on his shoulder, and walked the springy boardwalk to the saloon. Then he maneuvered through the crowd to get back to the piano, and she smiled up at him.

"Did you?" she asked.

"Your bathwater is growing cold."

With that, she hit a hard note on the keyboard for a finale, nodded to her cheering fans, and he led her through the aisle they made for her. Outside, she hugged him and laughed aloud. Her music had set her free again.

"When you coming back tah play again, lady?" a weaving drunk asked her.

She patted him on the check and winked. "One day."

At the suite door, Slocum swept her up in his arms and carried her inside the room. Holding her, he spun her around until he spotted the red roses in the vase on the dresser, and then he stopped.

She clasped both hands over her mouth and screamed, "Oh, my God, how did you do that?"

"I'll tell you later. That bathwater is cooling."

"Why, this room is big as a house." He set her down, and she looked so dreamy-eyed, he wondered if she would ever undress. First, she went and smelled the roses; then, she took one stem out of the vase and whirled around with it.

When she stopped, she blinked in disbelief at him. "Oh, yes, the bath is cooling, my lord."

They both laughed, and she quickly shed her cowboy clothing. Side by side in the steaming water, they laughed and washed.

"How many hours did you play?" he asked.

"I don't know—time means nothing when I am into it. I swim in the music until I grow tired of it or someone interrupts me. I don't see faces, though I know they are there. If they enjoy it, fine—I am immersed in it, you would say, and it makes me lighter than air. I once saw a Frenchman with a balloon float high over the Arkansas River. I know how he felt. My music does that better for me more than any drink or any compound I've ever tried."

"You hypnotize people with your music on an old tinny piano that no one else could extract those sounds from."

"We all have talents. I know a Cherokee who can carve small bears and horses so real, you expect them to run away."

"You sure paint pretty pictures with your music."

"Good," she said, and popped up in a rush of water that ran off her pale snowy skin. "I'll shave your face if you have a razor, and then we can see about that bed."

"It looks very high. We may need a ladder to get into it. The razor and brush are in my saddlebags."

After drying herself off, she found his razor in his saddlebags and soon had him seated in a chair. Lathering his face with his brush first, she began to ease the razor over his cheeks, swiping the whiskers and soap off the blade each time. With care, she cleared his upper lip, then the chin, and finally his neck. Her eyes glistened with excitement when she scrubbed his face clean with a wet towel and then dried it.

"Now." She made a bow and extended her hand and arm in the direction of the bed. "Your handmaiden awaits you."

He gathered her up in his arms and kissed her. Her warm clean skin against his—damn—damn, he would sure miss her when she was gone.

Morning came too soon, but he had two herds to see about. They ate breakfast in the hotel restaurant—fried eggs, ham, fried potatoes, biscuits with thick gravy. No grits were available. Just as well this far north. They couldn't cook grits right anyway. The coffee was strong and had good flavor, but two dollars apiece for breakfast—the price should have been fifty cents.

He found the crew on the road. Dawson McLain had found some good grazing where another herd had recently left, and it was close enough from there to easily drive the animals into Abilene. So, pleased with his own bunch, Slocum rode on south.

Victor meet him on the road that afternoon and agreed to find a place to hold that herd until they could move it up to where Slocum's herd was now.

"You sell 'em?" Victor asked.

Slocum nodded. "McClanahan paid me eleven cents plus one percent cut."

"You did well. Got more than I did. But you know, there are folks holding out for fifteen cents and they'll sure be here all winter. Why, I bet the damn snow will blow right up your asshole this far north."

"I know it will. I'm not wintering in Kansas either." Slocum shook his head.

"Fifteen cents is lots of money, but a bird in the hand beats a bird in the bush."

"Right. We're selling these cattle, too. I may have him on them. He seems to need them badly."

"More folks hold out, the better the market will be."

"You hold up and I'll get them sold quick as I can. Then move you in there where we are now."

They shook hands and Slocum headed for Abilene. it was damn near dark. His *bride* would be awaiting him.

Long past midnight, he dropped out of the saddle and handed the reins to the sleepy-eyed hostler at the livery. "Grain him when he cools out," Slocum said. And then he flipped him a dime.

When he came into the room, she was lying on the bed in a frilly dress with ruffles down the front. "Have you eaten?"

He shook his head and kissed her.

"We shall go eat then."

"You have something to eat?" he asked.

She smiled as he nibbled on her neck and held her tight against him, swinging her from from side to side. "I'm really not hungry," she said.

He laughed aloud. "I'll eat you then."

"Oh, that sounds heavenly."

"Baby, I have the energy to make love to you or go eat. Which do you want to do?"

Her finger poking him in his chest, she said, "You."

"Good. I adore this dress," he said, opening the numerous buttons down the front and then slipping it off her bare shoulders.

Next morning, he awoke and it was daylight outside. "What time is it?"

"I thought you needed some sleep," she said, coming over by the bed.

He swallowed hard and combed his hair back with his fingers. "I've got—"

She slipped like a mountain lion in front of him, then clutched his head against her stomach in the ruffles of her blue dress. "Oh, my impatient lover. You have all day. Tomorrow is when you will begin to load cattle. Stop worrying so much. Mr. Ryder's interests are being taken care of."

He raised up and looked into her face. "I guess you're right."

"Right?" She hiked her dress up to unbutton it from the bottom and revealed herself from the hem up. "I know I am right. Now, you just relax. I want my reign in this luxurious room to be one I won't forget."

In seconds, with her dress open, she quickly moved to sit astraddle his legs and kissed him with the heated desire of a prairie fire. The ropes under the bed squeaked with their fierce lovemaking. Her on top. Him on top of her. Her on her hands and knees underneath him. Finally, her sprawled facedown on the sheets with him driving his erection straight into her heart.

With her fist, she beat the mattress and sheets. "Yes. Yes."

Then he exploded inside her. They sprawled out in exhausted wonderment, cuddled in each other's arms. The only people in the world. Adam and Eve in the Garden of Abilene.

# 19

The cattle were coming. Part of Vic's crew was helping sort, and a couple more hands with horses that needed work were helping. Five hundred an hour was the way McClanahan wanted them. Weighed, then loaded in the pens and poked with long sticks into the cars. Horns cracked together. Dust boiled up in a cloud over the pens, mixed with the bitter coal smoke from the donkey locomotive moving cars to and from the ramps.

The weights looked good. Slocum decided they might average eight hundred pounds. That meant eighty-five dollars per steer. Ryder's gross income could be over a hundred fifty thousand dollars. The notion of that much money staggered Slocum. Why, Ryder would be one of the richest men in Texas. Herds all summer had been coming up here—selling like that.

Slocum shook his head in amazement as the next group of steers crowded on the scale.

"Twenty-one head?" the weight master asked him, verifying the number on the scale.

Looking them over, Slocum reviewed the count, then stepped off the scale. "Yes, sir."

By dark, they'd have the cars loaded. McClanahan was taking the Travis brothers' herd at ten cents a pound with a two-percent cut. It was the best he could do. Their cattle were not as uniform as Ryder's herd. There were several older cattle among them, and some even younger. McClanahan said the brothers' herd was typical of most herds, some of which even had yearlings in them that he had no market for, and cows as well.

While the cattle deal was being settled, Slocum's musical delight was moving about town gathering information on any man with bells on his boots.

Slocum met her in Claude's Diner for lunch. They ordered the plate lunch—sliced beef, mashed potatoes, and fresh green beans with coffee.

"Learn anything today?" he asked.

"Yes. A gambler named Routh who seems to fade in and out of here. Folks say he is very tough with a short temper. He also carries on his horse, in a special holster, a cut-down twenty-gauge shotgun that has been made into a pistol."

Slocum wet his lower lip and nodded. "I think he's our man. You know where his base camp is?"

"North, I think."

"Wire the Travis brothers in San Marcos after lunch. Tell them we have their cattle sold at a fair price. Sale will be done late this week. And ask them the brand on their horses and mules."

"What will the brand do?"

"Routh might still have some of them. A brand could prove a lot."

A smile crossed her thin lips and her dark eyes twinkled. "You should be the law."

"No, I simply want justice for those ambushed cowboys, and that Routh and his gang don't do anyone else like that."

"I'll send it off right after lunch. What else?"

"Find out where he's got a camp or farm at. But be very careful. The man is a killer."

She agreed, and their food arrived.

When they completed lunch, she pecked him on the cheek and swirled out of the cafe in the new black dress that he'd sent her to buy. He went back to the cattle weighing at the scale house—Ryder better get ready to pay him a bonus.

"I'll give you a receipt for the cattle today, and we will meet at the Merchant's and Cattleman's bank on Friday in the morning and I'll issue you the drafts there for all the cattle," McClanahan said.

Slocum nodded. He couldn't let anything go wrong. These two sales would amount to more money than he could even imagine.

Who was this Routh? Was there any way to tie him to the raid on the Travis brothers' herd? It had to be a brand. No one knew Dawson McLain up there. Maybe if McLain rode up there and scouted around north of town, looking to buy some horses for a drive he was going to make to Nebraska, he could find Routh's outfit. But even better, buy a horse or mule with a brand on it that Routh's outfit had stolen.

He'd have to talk to McLain by himself about spying on Routh. His man could do that without too much risk. By the time they got the cattle weighed and loaded, Belle might even have found where Routh and his bunch hung out.

By dark, with the last steer loaded, he knew they'd lost less than five percent of the cattle. They had 1,922 head. Sitting in the weight master's shed, they pored over the weight tickets.

"They average eight-twenty-seven apiece," McClanahan said, poking the pencil behind his ear and sitting back in the squeaking chair.

The weight master, Jenks, agreed.

The cattle buyer leaned over and did some calculating on a scrap of paper on the desk. "Those steers averaged eighty-six dollars and eighty-three cents apiece. What will your boss think of that?"

"I suppose he'll think he's rich."

Exhausted, with a loud sigh, McClanahan dropped both

his arms down beside the chair. "Day after tomorrow we start on the Travis brothers' herd."

"You have the cars?" Jenks asked him.

"Oh, yes. I'll have them here day after tomorrow. I hope those greedy bastards out there that are holding out for fifteen cents freeze their fucking asses off this winter."

"You acted awfully nervous the first day I met you," Slocum said, tenting his fingers in front of his nose. "You kinda worried me."

McClanahan nodded. "I had a drover I'd made a deal with that flat backed out on me. They won't get fifteen cents next spring for them either. I had cars coming. I had orders to buy cattle. I was nervous, but I can't pay you more than they'll pay me back East."

"I savvy that. Now, day after tomorrow, we load the Travis brothers' cattle?"

"Oh, yes, we have a deal. But they're not near as good overall as the cattle you brought in for Ryder."

Slocum leaned back in his swivel chair and pointed his tented fingers at the man. "I'm learning. Learning a lot. Load those cattle Thursday, and settle for both herds on Friday. They have that much money here?"

The cattle buyer smiled, laughed, and dismissed his concern with a wave of his hands. "They do."

"Good. I'll be anxious to get back to Fort Worth." He probably wouldn't sleep a wink going back, thinking about how much money he was carrying back with him to Texas.

"I better get a bath and see about the lady," Slocum said, getting up to leave.

"When's she doing another concert?" Jenks asked.

Slocum stopped in the doorway and turned back. "She hasn't told me when."

Both men laughed.

Victor sat his horse in the gathering sundown outside the scale house. He dismounted at the sight of Slocum coming through the door.

"Something wrong?" Slocum asked.

"No, we're bedded down on your old ground. Things are ready for the morning. I just wanted to talk to you a minute about a deal."

Slocum looked around and, satisfied they were alone, nodded for him to go ahead.

"There's an outfit from California that's been delivering gold safely for years called Wells Fargo. Bad as these crooks and road agents are, I shipped my cattle proceeds by them to San Antonio."

"Who did you ship to down there?"

"Southwest Cattleman's Bank accepted the money and put it in a vault for my boss to claim."

"Sounds great. Where can I make arrangements?"

"They'll help you at the bank here. Of course, there's a hefty fee."

"Thanks, Vic. I was thinking that much money and word always gets out—" Slocum shook his head.

"I felt the same way. Any news on the killers?"

"Belle's got some leads. And a name. Routh?"

"Who's he?"

"Gambler and trader, I think. He's pretty tough and carries a twenty-gauge pistol that I think killed most of those cowboys."

"Sounds serious."

"Oh, any man who killed over a dozen hands in cold blood would be tough or crazy."

"Yes, he would be. I'll let you go. We hadn't discussed a firm handling that money, but I think it would be lots easier to let them do it than hauling it back yourself."

"I'll wire Ryder and the Travis brothers and tell them how the proceeds are coming."

They parted, and Slocum took the stairs two at a time after ordering up a bathtub and hot water from his man Elmer.

"Halfway done," she said, smothering herself against him when he came in the room.

"My bath is coming. That scale job is worse than riding drag with the dust and damn coal smoke."

"Guess what I learned today."

He looked down at her. "What did you learn?"

"His name is Lee Roy, two words, Routh. His main man's name is Charlie Watts, and he's got three Indian half-breeds and a one-eyed fella named Toolie on his payroll."

"Where do they hole up?"

"On the Republican River north of here. West of the road that goes to Nebraska. He makes and sells whiskey to Indians and, I guess, white men."

"You found all that out today?"

"Whorehouses have thin walls—"

A knock on the door. Slocum went across the room and opened it. With Elmer overseeing the help, they delivered a copper tub, and three ample-bodied housekeepers brought in buckets of steaming water. Slocum tipped them all and after a bow, they left.

When he was in the tub at last, Belle scoured his back with a long-handled brush. Then used her yucca soap shampoo to wash his hair.

He told her about Victor's suggestion, and she agreed.

"How much money is it?" she asked him.

"After we pay the help and I get my bonus, over one hundred fifty thousand dollars."

She threw her head back and then looked in wide-eyed shock at him. "That much?"

"That much."

Slowly, she nodded. "I heard that a few trail bosses took the proceeds and ran away with it. My heavens, that is more money than I could count."

"It's why I think those fools out there holding out for higher prices are dumb. Take the money and run home."

"I agree."

"I'm going to have Dawson go up and see if he can find out anything about the Travis horses up north. They won't know him and maybe we can learn something."

She agreed, ready with a towel to dry him off. "Will you use the law?"

He shook his head. "Aside from that tough town marshal, there is no real law up here."

"Let's dine in the hotel tonight. I feel like something fancy."

Busy dressing in a second set of clothes she'd bought for him, he agreed.

The supper was very elegant, and Slocum could see his lady knew all about such meals. He left the details to her, and enjoyed watching her in action.

"This bread is fresh that you are bringing us, isn't it?" she asked the waiter.

"Ah, yes, madam. Fresh from the oven. Still hot and easy to slice."

"Splendid."

Amused, he sat back and studied her. The lady from seventy miles west of Fort Smith down on the Canadian River. Mrs. Cole Younger. *Younger, I am damn sure enjoying you sharing your wife with me.*

"What's so funny?" she asked.

"Nothing and everything, my dear."

She looked around, then satisfied that no one could hear her, said through her teeth, "Wait until I get you in bed. It won't be so damn funny then."

They both laughed.

He rose early, left her sleeping, then talked the waitress in the small café out of a quick cup of coffee and a pocket full of fresh biscuits to eat on the way. He knew all the hands were up at Vic's camp and he wanted to catch McLain.

Coalie and Goody were really putting out the food. They'd traded a farm wife out of enough eggs for a leg of beef they'd killed to feast on for days. One of those other folks' cattle, Coalie assured Slocum, and they all laughed.

The eggs proved a big treat, and the boys were taking bites of them on their forks. "Look, real eggs."

"There are still chickens in America," another put in.

"I thought a hawk ate 'em all," another puncher said.

At last, Slocum got McLain alone and they talked. He agreed to ride up north and "buy some horses." Slocum gave him a hundred dollars. "Only buy the TB-branded ones. And be careful, they're killers and bad ones."

"I like this ole earth, Boss Man. I'll be careful."

"You find any TB horses, the Travis brothers, I'm certain, will reward you."

"Hell, I'd just like to get those killers."

"I'll tell Vic you are running errands for me. Take your bedroll. You may be out there for a few days. I'm staying at the Cattleman's Cottage Hotel."

"I'll find you. Tell Miss Belle we sure miss her music in the cow camp."

"She says she plans to go back with all of us."

"Good. I love her music. See you soon as I find out anything."

"Dawson, this ain't worth losing your life over. We can get those fellas. This needs to come off easy or get the hell out of there."

"I understand."

"Make sure you do." Slocum counted on him knowing that. He'd lost enough people. Bonner being shot down for being a Confederate. Pike killing himself over the complexities of things. The whole Travis crew murdered.

Slocum spoke to Vic before he rode out for town. "McLain is running some errands for me. Guess you and the crew are ready for tomorrow."

"The boys been asking. She's going back with us?"

Slocum smiled. "She says she is."

"That'll make their day. I'll tell them. They love her music." Vic grinned big.

Slocum waved adios and rode back to Abilene.

When he dismounted at the livery across the street, he saw the breed wrapped in a blanket who noted his arrival and then turned to leave. His heart stopped for a second. *There are three breeds up at Routh's camp.* Those were Belle's words. He gave the hostler the reins and, dodging traffic, ran across the street to where he'd last seen the breed. Then, he slipped down the narrow passageway between the buildings.

At the back of the buildings, he saw the breed talking to a man on horseback. The rider wore a high-crown top hat and buckskin clothing, and was one-eyed. What was the breed telling One-eye while he sat on the buffalo pony with its ears half cropped off?

Maybe Belle had asked too many questions about them? Damn, he better go see about her next. Then One-eye whirled the paint around and raced out of Abilene toward the north. Was he going after his boss, or to tell his boss about Slocum's arrival in Abilene?

Slocum would probably do no good beating the crap out of that buck. He wouldn't tell him a thing after Slocum mopped up the alley with him. But if they knew that McLain worked for Slocum . . . That was something to worry about after seeing that meeting between those two hard cases who acted awfully interested in Slocum being in Abilene.

Damnit to hell anyway.

# 20

Back at their hotel room, Slocum shared his concerns about Routh and his henchmen and breeds on his payroll with Belle.

"I wear my pistol everywhere I go," she said. "I can use it."

"I know you can but I don't want you in some gunfight. I get those cattle of the Travis brothers weighed and sold, we're sending the money south and going home—well, after I settle with Routh."

"A couple of blanket-ass half-breeds are of no concern to me." In his arms, she looked up and scoffed at the notion.

"Belle, I think you may have struck a nerve somewhere asking folks too much about them."

"Or they think that you are getting the money from the sale of two herds and they want all of it."

"Holy cow, that could be it. The proceeds from the two herds will sure enough be lots of money. And they may have made plans to go back and gather that Travis herd later and sell it themselves."

"You never gave them the chance to take control of it. First, our boys began to gather the cattle and took charge. Then, I hired Vic for you, and he'd be a tough one to buck."

"He would be. But one big robbery like that would set a man like Routh up for life."

"The sale of that Travis herd with the money in his pocket would do that."

He hugged her tight. "Keep your gun handy. We aren't done yet."

"Tomorrow we sell the second herd, and I have telegrams from both owners," she said. "They like the idea of Wells Fargo shipping the money to them."

"Good."

"Read the Travis brothers' telegram." She went to the dresser for it.

MY BROTHER AND I CANNOT THANK YOU
AND YOUR PEOPLE ENOUGH   THIS SALE IS
GOING TO SAVE OUR LIVES AND RANCH
PAY WHO YOU NEED TO AND BE SURE TO GET
YOUR PART FROM THE PROCEEDS   COME BY
THE RANCH ANYTIME   GOD BLESS YOU

"Serious business getting cattle to market when so much rides on it," he said, putting the paper down.

"What will you do with your share?"

"I have no idea."

"We should buy some of that rich farmland down on the Canadian River and hire us a good farmer to work it on the shares. Tight as money is, you could buy some real good land."

"Buy a corset for the trip back."

"Do I need one?" She looked vexed at him.

"No, you don't need one, but we do, so we can sew our money in it."

She broke up, laughing. "Well—I'll just be a traveling bank."

"And maybe I can make deposits in it."

"Oh, please do." Then they went off to lunch.

After lunch, she left him to find the right corset while

he played nickel-dime poker in Stauffer's Bar. Several of the fifteen-cents-a-pound crowd were in there complaining. Slocum ignored them until one man made a rather pointed comment at him.

"Why did you sell?" he demanded.

"The people owned the cattle told me to sell. Hell, they ain't mine."

"They realize that five cents a pound is forty dollars on these big steers?"

"Mister, most of these people are so broke they can't even think."

The man scowled at him. "They're the ones depressing the damn market."

"Talk to them. I just work for a living."

"Weren't you the one gathered up that herd where they shot the whole crew?"

Slocum nodded.

"Never got the killers?"

"No, but they'll show up. When I find them, will you boys help me serve a little justice?"

"How will you prove it?"

Slocum cut the man a sharp gaze. "When I get the evidence, you won't doubt it."

"Mister, there ain't been an arrest made yet, and that ain't the first herd where the crew was shot and the herd vanished."

"Yeah," another put in. "Bill Wolf's boy from down by Denton crawled in here last spring saying their herd was stolen and all of them were dead. Ain't been one gawdamn arrest yet."

"Oh, they're smooth, but they ain't that smooth," Slocum said. "Give me your names if I need a posse."

The names flew—Combs—Regis—Walton—Comer—Tanks—Shepherd—and Thomas.

"When will you know?" Walton asked.

"By dawn or shortly thereafter. Deal the cards," Slocum said to Tanks, whose turn it was.

"We'll just wait up then."

The clock over the back bar struck one A.M. Slocum looked up and saw Belle coming through the door with McLain behind her.

"Thought you'd be asleep, so I went by the hotel," the cowboy said apologetically.

A silence settled over the room and men strained to listen.

"You find the evidence?" Slocum asked loud enough that everyone could hear him.

McLain nodded. "The Travis brothers' mules are in their camp. They sold me three cow ponies that have the TB brand on them."

"Is Routh in camp?"

"Yes. I bought them from Routh himself."

An angry murmur went through the room.

"We'll get our horses and guns and be ready to ride in thirty minutes." Old Man Combs spit out his tobacco into an overflowing spittoon. "It's time there was law spelled out in this country."

A loud amen came from the other men.

Belle stood back, chewing on her lower lip. Slocum motioned for her to come forward.

"That's what you wanted, wasn't it?" she asked, looking uncertain.

He hugged her shoulder. "You stay here."

Woodenly, she agreed. "I'm going to play. You be careful." Then she headed for the piano.

"Ma'am, you can't play that piano. The boss said only—"

The bartender's words were cut off when a great knife was waved in his face by a large Texas drover. "That's Miss Belle. I say she can play it. Where's your boss at right now?"

"Ah—ah, asleep."

"Then we won't wake him with the news of your death."

"No, sir."

*Rock of ages, cleft for me* . . . Her music carried down the dark street as Slocum and McLain walked to the livery to get McLain a fresh horse and to saddle Slocum's own.

In thirty minutes, nearly two dozen armed men and their horses were in the street, ready to ride.

"It's important we don't shoot each other," Slocum said, and drew some laughter. "I'll give the command. These are tough criminals. Three are breeds. The man in charge uses a shotgun pistol. We will come in from three sides. The fourth side is the Republican River and while shallow, according to my man, it should slow up any flight that way."

Slocum pounded the horn on his saddle. "I want none of us hurt. So be careful and don't rush in. Everyone understand?"

"Yes," came the chorus.

He turned his horse around to leave, listening to Belle's music. *Amazing grace, how sweet the sound that sav'd a wretch like me!*

# 21

A banty rooster crowed as the outlaws were kicked out of their bedrolls by the rifle-bearing posse men. A big man that Slocum suspected was Routh offered them some resistance, and a rifle butt slammed in his back drove him to his knees.

"Who's in charge?" the man demanded, staggering to his feet.

Slocum drove his horse in that direction. "I'm in charge."

Men moved aside as they forced Routh towards Slocum.

"Who in the fuck are you?" Routh asked.

"I'm the agent for the Travis brothers. Yesterday, my man Dawson McLain bought three horses stolen from their cavvy on the night that their herd crew was murdered. There are four mules here with the TB brand, a mark registered to the Travis brothers in San Marcos, Texas."

"You can't prove I stole them. This is Kansas, not Texas. Besides, you aren't the law here."

"Routh, do your spurs have bells on them?"

"Sure. What the hell is that to you?" He stood, arms folded over his chest, defiant and acting like Slocum and his men were the invaders and trespassers.

"A dying cowboy testified to me that his killer wore silver bells on his spurs."

"Everyone has them."

"No, they have jingle bobs, Routh."

"Aw, you fellas better go on now and mind your own damn business."

"No, Routh. We are your judge and jury. This is a democracy. How many of you men want to take him into Abilene to stand trial?"

Wind rattled the coin-sized leaves in the tall cottonwoods. A hen, freshly separated from a new egg, ran off cackling her news. Some horse snorted in the dust.

"All right who says we hang them?"

A roar went up, and Slocum waited until they quieted down. "Justice will be served here then. Tie their hands behind their backs, seat them on the ground, and a few of you go saddle some horses. Any of you can tie a noose—" He began to count the outlaws. Three breeds, One-eye, a short crippled man, a kid who stood crying, and Routh.

Slocum walked over to the cripple on crutches. "What's your name?"

"Charlie Watts."

"What's your part in this business?"

The man shrugged.

"You better answer me. My patience is short this morning."

Watts's eyes narrowed. "Go to hell, you sumbitch."

Slocum nodded. "I'll see you there."

Then he went over to the youth. "How old are you?"

"Seventeen."

"What's your name?"

"Ivory Means."

"Empty your pockets."

When Slocum saw the gold pocket watch, he stopped him. "I guess you bought that watch."

The boy sniffed and shook his head, unable to staunch the tears pouring down his cheeks.

"You got that off a man that you killed or helped kill, didn't you?"

"Yes, sir." Sniff.

"Then, Ivory, you better get down on your knees and pray to your God to take you in heaven 'cause we're hanging you like the rest of these killers." Heads of the posse members nodded in agreement.

"Oh, no!" the boy wailed.

Slocum said to the men, "Get that contraband off all of them." Then he walked away.

Within thirty minutes, seven bound figures sat in their saddles, the ropes slung over three large tree limbs. The nooses were set beside their left ears to snap their necks when they fell off the animals underneath them.

Seven posse men stood with coiled-up lariats, ready to bust the butts of the ponies in front of them when the signal was given. Birds chirped in the trees. The day's wind had picked up, rustling the leaves louder.

"Now!" Slocum shouted.

Horses busted away. The outlaws were swept off their seats and the ropes made a loud tightening sound when their loads fell—hard. Most of their necks snapped. But not before several of them defecated in their pants. The foul smell hung in the air even with the wind. One of the breeds strangled, and he took several minutes to suffocate.

Slocum turned to McLain. "Get the Travis brothers' horses and mules out of that herd. I'm coming." He swung in the saddle and shouted, "Put all the contraband and money you find into sacks and anonymously give it to some church in town for the poor. It's blood money and maybe the church can cleanse it.

"See any horses that you know their owners, you can return them. Leave the rest at the livery for resale if unclaimed."

"This will be a better land without these devils," Walton said. "Slocum, we're grateful for your help, ain't we, boys?"

"Yes."

"No need to talk about it. It's done and it's over. But it may serve notice on the ones that prey on others. There is justice in Kansas."

"Amen."

He rode over to help McLain gather the horses and mules. In a short while, they had them headed for Abilene. Fifteen ponies and four good mules. Only part of the remuda was recovered, but the mules were the important part. They could haul the chuck wagon stored down at Wichita Crossing back to Texas.

Bleary-eyed, Slocum and McLain penned them at the livery. McLain rolled out his bedroll there in the haystack to catch some sleep, and Slocum shuffled back to the hotel. Belle was gone—somewhere. He toed off his boots, shed his britches and shirt, then flopped on the bed and slept hard.

He didn't wake up until he heard her singing some hymn. Fighting his way up from the deep sleep, he sat on the edge of the bed, mopping his face with his calloused hands.

"You forget about McClanahan?" she asked.

"Oh, shit—"

"It's all right. I told him I'd have you there at four thirty."

"What time is it now?"

"A little after four."

"I'll dress," he said, reaching for his shirt.

"Here's your safety-deposit box." She held up a new white corset. "I had the seamstress make the pockets for it."

"Wonderful. I need a list of who I need to pay and how much."

"I did all that on paper while you were asleep."

He shook his head in amazement. "We are a team."

"And a damn good one. What about Routh?"

"Him and his bunch are roasting in hell."

"I thought so."

He soon was dressed, stomping on his boots. "Let me get my hat and we'll go meet McClanahan."

"Have you been thinking any more about a bottomland farm down there?" she asked.

He squeezed her shoulder. "Sounds good to me."

"Really?"

"Yes."

She snuggled against him. "You are a wonderful man."

"But I am not going to farm it. You will be in charge."

"Sure."

He read the figures on the paper she'd given him as they walked toward the bank, and he whistled. "You mean that at five percent on both herds, we have almost fourteen thousand dollars, plus my salary?"

She nodded. "I did the calculations four times."

He lowered his voice. "Even with their losses and expenses, the Travis brothers will get a hundred thousand dollars. Yes, they will be happy."

She looked up and winked. "I paid the drovers on our crew for an extra month and Victor's for two months."

"Yes, I agree they all deserve it." He opened the bank door, and McClanahan got out of a chair in the lobby, a smile on his face.

"The first trainload is there and no losses," McClanahan said.

"Good. The killers are gone, too," Slocum said under his breath.

"Very good."

The three were escorted into an office behind frosty windows. A banker named Weldon Norman handled the papers, smiling several times at Belle. The checks for the full amount were written and signed by McClanahan, and Slocum endorsed them.

"Here's my list of expenses for each transaction," Slocum said. "They are separate and I want them in cash."

"This a sizable sum," Norman said, looking at the amount.

"It costs money to move cattle. Then, I want the money specified sent separately by Wells Fargo to the Southwest Cattleman's Bank in San Antonio to be held in safekeeping for the claimants or me."

"We can handle that for a service fee of three hundred dollars for each account."

Belle looked shocked, and about to protest.

Slocum shook his head at her. "That includes Wells Fargo's fee?"

"Yes, sir."

"Show that cost along with these expense accounts that go with each one."

Norman nodded. "I will give you a receipt for both of them, and my clerk will make a copy of these neat invoices to include with the money. Did you do them, sir?"

"No, Belle did them. She's very well educated."

"Ma'am, if I may say so, your piano concerts are wonderful. I could listen all night to you playing."

"Thank you," she said demurely.

"You will excuse me?" McClanahan asked, standing up and tipping his hat to her. "You're a good person to do business with—both of you. I seldom have anyone this organized to deal with. You have another herd coming, you telegraph me ahead of time. I want them if they're as good as the first ones."

"Have a good night. I may be back." Slocum shook his hand and the cattle buyer left them. Norman was gone to get the cash that Slocum would need to pay his crew and buy her bottomland farm.

"Think it will all fit in my—corset?" she whispered.

Slocum chuckled. "You may be the sweet little chunky girl wearing it."

She slapped his arm.

Norman returned and stacked the money on the counter. "I hope you have some armed guards to protect you."

"We do," Belle said, and showed him the pearl handed pistol she wore at her waist.

Norman swallowed hard and nodded.

After Norman finished counting the money for them, Slocum thanked him and excused him from the office. Belle quickly shed her dress, and Slocum undid the strings to her underwear. In no time, the stack of money for his bonus, rounded off to fourteen thousand, was packed in her corset. Then he placed their salaries in a money belt he put back around his waist.

She looked at the ceiling, slipping her arms into the weighted corset. "I may be that chunky girl after all."

He kissed her on the cheek and then he began lacing the corset up in back.

"Do you know people who rob banks never get this much money from them?" she asked.

"They must rob poor banks," he said. They laughed as he tied the strings off.

"I never thought about that. Poor banks. That is funny."

They rode out to their outfit's chuck wagon, and set up boards on wooden horses for a table. Coalie brought them canvas chairs. The drovers were seated about the area on the ground, joking and laughing.

Slocum called off each man's name and he got up, came over, and Slocum counted out the money. "We paid you for an extra month 'cause you boys did so much."

"Well, I sure thank you, Boss Man," Blister said.

The others shouted thanks, too. When it was Dawson McLain's turn, Slocum stopped before counting out his money.

"Dawson, you're the new trail boss going home. I'll be there, but you pick campsites, settle disputes. You're in charge."

A smile and nod went with Slocum's handshake. Then McLain signed his name to indicate that he'd received the money listed on the sign-out sheet.

Belle carefully crossed their names off her list as Slocum paid them, consulting with him about each amount.

Victor and his men had ridden over by this time. They were next to be paid.

"We've paid all of you for two months work," Slocum

told them at the start. "You saved us and the Travis brothers' herd. They said to thank everyone. At that distance, they could have lost everything."

Slocum looked at the boy who had had the experience earlier with the ugly whore. "You going to try again?"

"No! I'm keeping this money and going home with it." His face turned red as a beet, realizing Belle was sitting there as he knifed the money down in his pants pocket.

"Vic, you know I appreciate all you did on such short notice," Slocum said when the man was the last to step up. "We hope this covers your expenses."

"It will. Enjoyed it. Sorry I didn't make that necktie party."

"We went up there without much notice."

"No problem. I'm just glad they're where they're at."

"So am I."

"Food's on!" Coalie shouted. "Everyone eats here tonight."

For the first time, Slocum noticed Sadie in her too-large apron wielding a spoon over a large pot to dip out something for the crew. She had a big smile on her face and ribbons in her hair, and she spoke softly to the hands, filling their plates.

"How's she doing?" he asked Belle.

"Quite well. She's going back to Texas with all of us."

"Good."

"Maybe you can find some stray dogs, too," Belle teased him. "I'll get you a plate."

He leaned back and stretched his arms over his head, at last feeling freer since it was all over. "Thank you."

Victor stopped by with his plate heaped high with food. "When're we leaving?"

"Day after tomorrow when the crew sobers up enough not to fall off the wagon."

"I'll be ready."

"Sit down. I'll find a keg."

"Naw, you and her—"

"She loves company. Stay." Slocum went to find a nail keg and brought it back.

Belle had returned with two plates and was talking to Vic. "It should be fun going home. No cattle to drive, right?"

"Oh, yes. Get to sleep every night. That will be the best part."

"You have a wife and family in Texas?" Slocum asked him.

"Yes, sir. My teenage son is making crops this year along with two hired hands. I hope they've had enough success at it so we can eat and feed our stock."

"Good."

"What will you do next?" Vic asked Slocum.

"Excuse me. Mr. Slocum, are we free to go to town, sir?" Rube asked.

"Go on, but be careful. We leave here day after tomorrow."

"Oh, we will. We really will," Rube said. "He says we can go, boys."

They left like wild men in a cloud of dust. Coalie, Goody, and Sadie were sitting on small stools finishing their supper when Slocum dropped by.

"I forgot you were on the payroll, Sadie, but Belle told me I owed you fifty dollars for putting up with these two galoots."

"Oh, my—I—I only helped—"

"Now, Sadie, don't go to taking back water, you sure earned that money," Coalie said. "You helped me and Goody a whole lot."

"She sure did," Goody said.

"Well, thank you, Mr. Slocum. You all are some of the nicest people I ever met in my life, and thank Miss Belle, too."

"You're going back to Texas with us?"

"If I can, sir."

"You may. Thanks. We'll be going back to Abilene and sleep in a hotel bed for one more night."

"Guess we plan on hitting it at daylight day after tomorrow?" Coalie asked.

"Yes. I have a feeling they'll be lots of drovers can't sit a horse and we'll need to load them in wagons."

"We can do it, sir. We know how."

He and Belle started back to Abilene alone.

"Guess we can afford another bath?" she asked.

"Sure, all the baths we want."

"I'm sure going to miss this honeymoon suite."

"Guess we've had one here."

"And there, and even back in Arkansas. It's been one big one for me." She shook her head. "Whew, me and that French balloonist have sure been flying."

"Me, too," he said, and they began trotting their horses.

He ordered baths sent up, and ordered some champagne as well. She was already halfway up the stairs and never heard Slocum order the last item. He winked at Elmer.

"I can sure handle it, Mr. Slocum."

Water, bathtubs, towels, and a bucket with ice and a bottle in it soon arrived.

"Should I open it, sir?" Elmer asked as she frowned at what he was up to.

"Certainly." Slocum moved beside her. "I have no balloon to fly in, but they do sell good French champagne in this town."

She giggled. "What does it taste like?"

"Bubbly."

She jerked back at the sharp report of the cork, and quickly Elmer poured the champagne into two long-stem glasses and served them.

"Hmm, it has bubbles all right," she said, holding the glass up to the room's light.

"Thanks, Elmer," Slocum said and hustled him out the door with a two-dollar tip.

When the door was closed and she was busy sipping, Slocum smiled. How wild could a mink get? He'd find out this night.

"It tickles your nose. The bubbles." She began to undress, until at last he had to undo the strings on her underwear.

They soon were in the tubs and she was well into her second glass. "This is dandy stuff."

Washed, she rose and water sheeted off her well-proportioned body. She dried herself; he dried himself. Then he dried her back and played with her tits. She moved like smoke, turning to face him.

"Tonight will be the best night we ever had," she said.

"How do you know that?"

"I can feel it." She rubbed her muff against his upper leg. He reached down and let his finger comb through her pubic hair. She set her bare feet farther apart for him to do more, and their mouths melted together in hunger.

His finger soon teased her swollen clit and she gasped for her breath. "Don't be long." Her voice was like the whisper of wind across the sand. Nipples turned rock hard buried in his hard, corded belly, her eyes squeezed shut, and she pulled him down to whisper. "Oh, dear God, take me to bed."

He swept her up in his arms after she finished her glass of bubbly. He laid her down on her back, and she raised her legs high and wide for his entry. With him on his knees between her legs, he held his rod and rubbed the head of his dick on her gates to tease her some more. She squirmed and moved herself closer to it as if anxious for his entry. But he felt like being ornery, and teased her with a quick in and out until she rose off her back.

"Oh, please don't tease me anymore. I need him so bad."

He agreed and moved forward. When he popped his throbbing erection inside her, she cried out, "Yes!"

He was on top, under her, and over her in the next twenty minutes or so. His chest ached for more air as he pounded her ass. She wheezed like a wind-broken horse. With her rock-hard buns nested in his flanks, he poked his stiff dick into her tight cunt from behind and played with her breasts underneath her. Then something passed over him like a shadow, and he pressed in her as deep as he could go. Out of nowhere, the hard cramp in both of his nuts exploded out the end of his dick, and she collapsed facedown in the pillow.

"Oh, my God," she moaned. "I have been torn apart."

"You bleeding?"

"How would I know? I can't see anything. Oh, I better open my eyes, huh?" Then she blinked at him. "I—I guess—I'm drunk."

He kissed her and fondled her half-hard tits. "Relax and sleep. I'll be here."

She patted his upper leg. "I—I'll—do that . . ."

Belle was out of it.

When she was asleep, he got up and drank the rest of the champagne out of the neck of the bottle while seated in a ladder-back chair. He stared at her naked form lying in a fetal position on the bed.

Strange, he'd never dreamed the job of driving cattle to Kansas was such a profitable operation. No wonder men risked life and limb to get there. How many crosses had he seen on the road north? Boys that would never see their mothers again. And their mothers could never decorate or even find their distant graves. *On the north bank of the Canadian River . . . the boss man said to her, then gave her her boy's wages and tipped his hat.*

He'd have Ryder do that for Bonner's people. As if the Texas families hadn't lost enough sons and fathers in the recent war, instead of enemy fire, now it was drowning, stampedes, lightning strikes, bad water, and horse wrecks that took them away.

And Belle Younger with a corset full of money to buy a bottomland farm. How long did he dare to stay? He'd used up some of his nine lives being in one deal this long. There was a knock on the door.

"Coming—" He jerked on his pants and unlocked the doors, easing it open a crack.

"Boss, it's me, Rube. McLain sent me. There's two deputy U.S. marshals circulating the saloons asking about you tonight."

"You sure it's me?"

"Yeah, John Slocum is who they want. Picture ain't much like you but they want you."

"What's their names?"

"Carr and Hamby."

Oh, shit. Two of the lawmen who'd confronted them at the cabin. Apparently, Carr was now a deputy U.S. marshal. "I'll give you some money," said Slocum. "Buy me a buggy and horse to pull it. Then drive it up to the back door of the hotel in the alley. Wait. I'll get you some money.

"Then I'll bring Belle down and drive out of here."

"I think I can do all that."

"You must get someone who isn't with us to send those two to Routh's old camp. And tell them if I ain't there, that I went on to Nebraska."

Rube nodded that he understood. "I'll do that first, then get the buggy?"

"Fine, but don't let them catch you."

"I won't."

"Good."

There was no waking Belle up, Slocum soon discovered. So he dressed her in the blue dress—it was the least valuable one. He put her other clothes and the corset inside the war bag. Then he ran downstairs on the quiet side and paid his bill with Elmer.

"If anyone asks about me—"

"They already did. I showed them the register that you weren't here. That Carr must not be able to read. He never saw your name, but it was a week-old page, too."

"I owe you, Elmer." After he paid their expenses, he gave the youth two twenty-dollar gold pieces. "Now run up and get my war bag. Belle drank a little too much bubbly, and I'll have to carry her down."

"Yes, sir. I sure didn't owe them dumb hicks anything."

Slocum about chuckled, and went upstairs to get her. With Belle slung over his shoulder, and Elmer taking two steps at a time going down ahead of him—he hoped that Rube had the buggy.

Like magic, the rig was at the back door and the drover was smiling. "I'll take your horses back to the outfit and you can catch us on the trail," said Rube.

"I will. You're a good man. Here, Elmer, put her things up here on the floorboard in front. They might fall out and when she comes to, she'd sure beat me if I lost them. Most of all, her valuable underwear."

"Where—we—going?" she moaned.

"To Texas. Hold on." With her head in his lap, he drove the fresh horse out of the alley and then south on the road for Wichita Crossing. The skin on the back of his neck crawled until he reached camp. Then Victor, who was already up drinking coffee, came over to see what was wrong.

"I need to catch her good horse out of the remuda and mine, too. Two deputy U.S. marshals have an old wanted poster for me and were passing it around last night."

"Holy cow, ain't you the lucky one."

"Yes."

"Slocum. Slocum," Belle screeched. "I wasn't ready to leave Abilene. And what in hell's name have you done with my corset?"

"I'll go get those horses for you." Vic was laughing as he mounted the night horse hitched to the wagon.

Slocum went back to the buckboard. "Hush up. It is in that war bag. We're at camp right now. Two of the lawmen who came to the cabin are back at Abilene looking for us. I have this buggy for you to drive. Vic's gone for our good horses."

"I'm sorry—baby—" Then she caught the buggy wheel for her support and bent over, vomiting.

"Miss Belle, that you? You bad sick?" Sadie came running with her skirt in her hand.

Belle waved her away as she clutched the wheel for support, and then she puked some more. "I'm fine—ugh."

When Vic returned, Slocum had an idea. "I need a big favor. Would you take Sadie in the buggy to Wichita Crossing? Then when folks see you go by, they will tell those two deputies they saw a couple going south. When those two deputies catch you, they will know you aren't us. We'll ride the back country with her dressed like a boy and meet you down there. It should throw them off."

Vic laughed, and when he finally stopped, he asked, "Sadie, will you go down there with me?"

"Why, I'd do anything you all need me to do, Mr. Vic. Sure I will."

Slocum had the extra saddles and pads on their horses, and he wondered if Belle could make it. Coalie was spoon-feeding her coffee, and Goody had some medicine that made her almost fight him when he gave her a dose.

Slocum helped himself to some hot fried side meat, and Sadie got him some biscuits out of the Dutch oven. Then she added some German fried potatoes to his plate.

"Will she eat anything?" Sadie asked, looking worried.

"Not for hours. Pack me some biscuits, dry cheese, and raisins. We can eat them on the road."

"Coalie made some fresh jerky while we've been camped. It's sure good."

"That'll do, too."

Sadie looked around to be certain they were far enough away from the others to talk. Then she asked in a low voice, "Will I look good enough to ride with him all the way down there?"

Slocum nodded. "He'll be proud of you."

"Oh, good."

"I need another horse to throw a packsaddle on," Slocum said to Vic. "I forgot all the stuff I have."

Vic mounted the right horse and went after another.

Shortly, he returned and Slocum tossed a pad and packsaddle on the bay pony. Vic dismounted and helped him. In no time, the bay carried their bedrolls, the war bag, and Belle's other things that he'd rounded up.

Belle had changed into men's clothing and was brushing out her hair. "Next time skip the champagne." Then she dropped her arms at her side. "I am still woozy."

"Better get over it. We have to ride."

"Slocum. The buggy exchange idea is neat. Those hicks won't figure it out ever."

"I hope not. I'll boost you up. You look weak."

Three days later, after dark, Slocum rode into their camp on the Arkansas at the crossing.

"What happened?" he asked McLain when he came to greet him.

"They caught up with Vic and Sadie out about ten miles north of here near the falls on Cottonwood Creek. Made 'em so mad they cussed a blue streak. Then they said that you must have gone to Nebraska and rode north."

"Good. I'll go get Belle."

"That's fine. We found a good fiddle some cowboy had hocked for two dollars. We'd sure love for her to play it for us."

"I imagine she will. Let me go get her."

When he returned for her, she came along playing "Ole Dan Tucker" on the mouth harp. *You're too late to get any supper . . .*

# 22

Nothing good in Slocum's life ever lasted very long, not even the taste in his mouth. On their return from Kansas late that long-ago summer, Belle used the cattle drive monies as a down payment for a large farm in the rich bottoms of the Canadian River—seventy-five miles southwest of Fort Smith at Younger's Bend, in that land assigned to the Starr family by the Cherokee Nation to settle a long-standing deadly feud between the tribe and the Starr's. At the time she considered Slocum her partner in the ranch.

Slocum drifted away shortly afterward. He went to the Southwest and other parts where he wasn't sought as hard by the law. A year or so later he heard she married Sam Starr's son. But he never forgot the dark-eyed Belle. At nights his dreams, when he was alone in his bedroll, were of making love to her, and even in bed with other women, he imagined they were her, that he was making love to her and not them.

A decade passed, and one day a rich man in Texas sent Slocum word he wanted him to find his son. Travis Boyd was the son's name. His daddy, a state senator, Elexus Boyd, had heard of Slocum and wired him a draft for two hundred dollars to come meet him in Austin and discuss finding the boy.

Slocum admired Boyd's handsome three-story house in the capital, the fine team of black trotters Boyd used for going back and forth to and from business as well as state senate sessions, and the matched grays he owned for other events. There was no telling what it all cost, Slocum thought as the educated black butler at the massive double front doors took his hat.

"Senator Boyd is in the library and awaits you, sir."

The paunchy well-dressed man sitting behind the polished desk in the library rose as Slocum entered the room. "John Slocum, I presume?"

"Slocum. Makes it easier to remember."

"Very well, Slocum, have a seat, sir. I must say, you are very punctual."

The large clock in the room struck two P.M.

"No problem." Slocum looked around at all the books neatly stacked in the room on shelf after shelf as he took a seat. "You read them all?"

"Most of them, unless they proved so boring I cared not to proceed."

"Some books are like that," Slocum agreed. "But when I complained to my late father about their lack of value, he made me read each one harder for one scrap of worth. I had to find that scrap before I could move on to the next book."

"Did you always find that scrap?"

"Yes. In the book I had the least use for, I told him the most valuable part was 'the end.'"

"Did he accept that?"

"He laughed at me and I was worried for a while, but he finally nodded and said, 'It must be a sorry book then.'"

"My son, sir. That's the reason I invited you here."

"You know where he is?"

"He's in western Arkansas—somewhere. I know that for I can trace him to there."

"For how long has he been gone?"

"Ten years."

"I guess he ran away?"

"Yes, he left after we had a bitter argument. He disappointed me and his late mother by marrying someone far beneath his class."

"How old was he?" Slocum tented his fingers and touched his nose.

"Oh, then twenty-five."

"Not a teenager?"

"No, but—"

"Senator, he left because you did not approve of his wife. At that age, he knew what he could do and did it. I am sure anyone could go up there and locate him. I doubt he's going to leave his wife and any children after all that time."

"Damnit, Slocum, he's my only heir. I have farms and ranches that he will inherit. I want to show him these places—" Boyd slipped down in the chair in great discomfort, breathing hard and his face pale. Slocum saw signs of trouble in the man's respiration.

He went to the door and called for the butler.

The man came running with prayers on his lips. "Sir, are you all right?"

Boyd seemed to be over the worst of it, and waved away the man who was now holding out a pill in one hand and a water glass in the other.

"Dr. James says you need to take one of these when you have those spells," said the butler.

"Spells—hmm."

"I will be close by if he has any more spells," the butler said to Slocum, and left the two of them alone.

Beads of sweat began to pop out on Boyd's forehead. He mopped his face with a white linen kerchief. Then the color began to rise red in his face again.

"My son doesn't have to like to me," said Boyd. "He can hate me. But for God's sake, convince him to come and take charge of what will be his."

"Why send me two hundred dollars for a fool's mission?"

Boyd closed his eyes. "Because I know you went to

Mexico and brought a man's rebellious daughter back. He sits in the Texas Senate with me. We talked about you at great length as the one person who could help me."

Slocum shook his head. This was not the same case. Jo Anna Warren was her name. A mild nymphomaniac who thought a Mexican bandit named Vaca was going to be her shining star. But Slocum drugged her, brought her back across the border, and then talked her into returning to her daddy's money. At eighteen, she was easier to convince after she saw the size of the cockroaches in Mexico. They were larger than Vaca's dick.

"I want you to try. I'll pay you five hundred to talk to him."

"I can say that I talked to him, collect my money after he says no."

"I don't care, but I'd pay you two thousand dollars if you can convince him to come back."

Slocum dried his palms on the top of his pants legs. "His low-class wife and kids included."

"She's a gawdamn blanket-ass Indian!"

"Settle down. Now, he ain't coming back alone. She's your daughter-in-law. You have to accept her or I'm not going. Those half-breeds are your grandchildren."

Boyd slumped in the chair. "All right. Bring them all. I can't say what I'll do."

"No, you will be civil to them."

"Damn you, Slocum. Warren told me you'd make me compromise like you did him."

"I don't care what I told Warren. He wanted his daughter back and wanted her to stay. We made that agreement after he stopped blowing off steam."

Boyd surrendered, holding up his hands. "I promise."

"Otherwise, he'll go back." Slocum waited for the man's response.

"I understand the terms. I will abide by them."

"I'll need some money wired to me if I make the deal. It costs bucks to move lock, stock, and barrel."

"Money is no object. If I die before you return, my law-yers know the circumstances and they will pay for every-thing. Bring him back. But I want to talk to him before I die."

"Pay me the two thousand dollars now."

"Why? You haven't got him yet."

"Boyd, if I don't get him, the money won't be any loss to you. But I might get shot on this mission and who would bury me?"

Boyd laughed. "I'll pay you, damnit. Get him to come home for God's sake."

"He'll be changed. Remember, he ain't the same boy that went up there."

On his knees at the open safe, Boyd drew out an enve-lope. With great effort, he rose to his feet unsteadily. Then he turned and tossed it on the desk. "Here is the money. Bring Travis home."

"I'll try, sir. Good day."

"Will I be hearing from you? And when?" Boyd shouted after him.

Slocum stopped at the doorway. "It'll be two weeks finding him up there. I'll try my best to get him to come back."

Using both hands for support on the top of the desk, Boyd said, "Telegraph me. That way, I'll try harder to live if he's coming."

"I can do that." Slocum left the man and let himself out of the house into the cool fall air. Train, stage, whatever, he'd head for Fort Smith and begin his search for Travis Boyd. The boy-turned-man was out there somewhere. He felt for the envelope on the inside of his coat pocket.

He'd earn this one.

# 23

A week later—mid-morning—on the boardwalk beside Garrison Avenue, he could hear a piano playing a hymn. He reached out and caught a black youth's shirt collar as he came running by. Then he swung him around to answer a question for him.

"Who's that playing that piano over there?"

"Why, *sah*, that sure be Miss Belle Starr. She just done got out of prison last week for horse stealing." A smile showed his even white teeth. "I's got to go tell a bunch of folks she's back and playing that piano in Dundee's Saloon. No telling how long she's going ta play. Now ain't she a real lady?"

"Yes, she is." Slocum paid the boy a shiny dime that made his muddy brown eyes sparkle and he thanked Slocum, leaving on the run again.

Dodging the traffic of beer wagons and freight wagons, carriages, horses, mules, and more bicycle riders, Slocum went across to the swinging doors and looked inside. There in the dim light, with her new cowboy hat brim pinned up by an ostrich feather, she clutched the keys and played. God how she could play. Her face had hardened over the last decade. Her eyes slanted more in the corners and she'd lost some weight. He'd call her too thin, but the simple sight of her still made his guts roil.

He considered turning away. She was married. Had she been to prison? What else?

"Come in, stranger," she said aloud to him and beckoned him over. "I may play a tune that you like."

He did so, and pulled up a chair close to her. Her audience stood three deep at the bar—quiet. They had been tapping their toes to the dance tunes, some singing the words to the hymns she played.

"Nice to see you," he said.

"Nice to be back here. Those Detroit prisons are dreary places."

"They said you were just released. I never knew you were in there, or I'd've tried something to get you out."

Still playing, she nodded as if considering his words. "It was our stupidity. It won't happen again."

"You've lost too much weight."

"The food up there is slop. I had no appetite." She began playing "Turkey in the Straw."

"You're married again?"

"I was the last time. What difference does that make?"

"Cole wasn't around then."

She wrinkled her nose and straightened her back playing the song harder. "Go around back behind Marie's Whorehouse. Go in the kitchen and tell her cook Ruby that you are a friend of Belle's and she'll show you to a room I can use. I'll be in there about five."

"How dangerous is that?"

"He'll be drunker than a hooter by then." She shook her head in dismay. "He don't give a damn."

"For old times?"

She smiled. "They really were special, weren't they?"

No way she'd ever know how special she had been to him. He nodded and rose, put the chair back. Then he left Dundee's and crossed Garrison Avenue.

Brad Jones ran a steam flour mill down between the docks and the railroad tracks. Slocum found the man, white with flour, working on his boiler's plumbing with two black handymen.

"Why, Slocum! What brings you up here?" Jones pulled off his gloves.

"A man in his thirties named Travis Boyd who married a full-blood. Where can I find him?"

"Boyd lives down in the river bottoms. Good man. What's he done?"

"Ain't what he's done. It's what I need to get him to do."

"What's that?"

"Go home and take over the family holdings in Texas. They're sizable."

They went into Jones's office, and the man shut the door against the noise of the mill works. "That shouldn't be hard."

"He's not poor, is he?"

"Naw, he's a good farmer. Why won't he go back?"

"Burnt bridges."

"Well, let me draw you a map to his place. It's nearly four. You want to go drink a few beers?"

"Another day, if your offer will be good." In an hour he had to meet Belle . . .

"For you, the offer is always open. Drop back by before you pull out. Oh, and good luck." They shook hands, and Slocum put the map in his pocket.

He took back alleys, side streets, and ended up squatted down in some cover behind Marie's two-story whorehouse to see if anyone had followed him. No one came. At last, he climbed the back steps and knocked.

A large black woman came to the door and looked at him skeptically. "You's ain't no salesman."

"Belle's expecting me."

"Oh, why you not say that right off?" She stuck her head out to look around, then quickly pulled him inside. "Right this way, sir."

She knocked on the door and a voice answered. "Let him in, darling."

With a wide grin and a wink, Ruby said, "She done be ready for you. My. My." Then she laughed and showed him inside, closing the door behind him.

Belle stood in the light coming through the multicolored shade trees in the yard and the sheer curtain material on the window. She was busy brushing her long hair. Tossing the brush aside, she rushed over into his arms. Holding her, he could feel her sharp shoulder bones. She was dressed in a blue gown like the one he recalled from their days gone by, and she hoisted the hem and began unbuttoning it.

His fingers trembled as he undid the buttons from the neck downward.

"You haven't taken any cattle to Kansas lately, have you?" she asked.

"Why? Are you short of money?"

"Yes. I spent almost two years in prison, and my share-croppers stole me blind and I owe taxes and haven't enough money to make the next crop."

He pushed the dress off her shoulder and bent over to kiss her right nipple. Like the rest of her, her breasts had shrunk, too, but fondling her still excited him. Already breathing hard, she opened his pants, felt for his genitals, and gently played with them. Their kisses grew stronger.

"Oh, my God, I dreamed of you taking me over and over again those damn nights in that damn prison. Get in bed." She ripped back the top cover and he began to undress.

Acorns set free by a gust of wind rattled off the roof. At last, he was between her thin legs, and then his dick was stuck inside her. It was her. It was her making love to him with wild abandon. Her—the woman he'd missed so badly all those years. His ass wanted to bore through her. They slipped in and out of positions until her contractions finally began and blew his mind. Then they did it twice more, and after the finale, the room was swallowed in darkness. It was night outside.

She went over, lighted a gas lamp, and came back to sit naked on the edge of the bed. "When can we do this again?"

He combed his hair back with his fingers. "We can't."

"But it was just like the old days. We make the best love together." She looked desperately at him. "Do you have a woman now?"

He shook his head and began to dress.

"Gawdamn you, Slocum! You just cannot walk out on me."

"How can I walk out on a woman that's married?"

"I can divorce him."

Dressed at last, he stood with his butt resting against the dresser. From inside his suit coat, he drew out the envelope and tossed it on the bed. "There should be enough money in there to save your farm."

"Why would you do that?" Her face looked concerned as she opened it to see the contents.

"The farm's part mine, I guess, and I don't want you to lose it."

She counted the money in the envelope, and soon tears began to run down her face in rivers. "Why are you giving this to me now and then leaving me?"

"I recalled a man once paid you half a debt, and then he wanted to screw you for him paying you. You said no to him. I figured if I gave that to you before, you'd never screw me."

"Damn you, Slocum. Where are you going from here?"

"I've got to earn that money I just gave you by convincing a man to go home."

"Will it be easy?"

"No. And if I fail, I guess the fella who paid me that money will have to sue me."

She waded across on her knees to his side of the bed. "Kiss me one more time—please."

He did and then he left the house.

Two weeks later, Slocum sat on the seat of the third new wagon headed down Garrison Avenue for the ferry. There were four wagons in the train, each heavily loaded, covered by new tarps, and with a dozen good-blooded horses in tow. When they halted at the Arkansas River's edge, Travis Boyd's handsome Cherokee wife came running back to talk to him. She stopped beside the wagon wheel, shading her eyes with her hands from the low midday sun's glare. Then, she stood on her moccasin toes and clutched the wheel's iron rim. "Did you hear that hymn back there that someone was playing in that saloon?"

Slocum fought back a knot in his throat, and finally swallowed it. "Yes. I heard it."

"My people sang that song on the Trail of Tears when they were driven out here. My grandmother told me about doing it. That's not a bad sign, is it? We aren't going on a sad trip, are we?"

He shook his head to dismiss all her fears. But a cold tear ran down his cheek anyway as he undid the brake ratchet to move his team of mules up to board the ferry.

*How great thou art . . . how great thou art . . .*